THE DEVIL'S BOSUN

H. BEDFORD-JONES

THE DEVIL'S BOSUN

H. BEDFORD-JONES

INTERIOR ILLUSTRATIONS BY

JAY McARDLE

ALTUS PRESS • 2015

© 2015 Altus Press • First Edition—2015

EDITED AND DESIGNED BY
Matthew Moring

PUBLISHING HISTORY
"The Devil's Bosun" originally appeared in the November 10 & 25, and December 10 & 25, 1935 issues of *Short Stories* magazine (Vol. 153 No. 3–6).

THANKS TO
Everard P. Digges LaTouche and Gerd Pircher

TABLE OF CONTENTS

THE TRUTH is revealed only in the sequence of events. You might think the meetings that morning on the bridge across the River of Gold were pure coincidence. They were not. Here was a gathering of forces, a culmination of schemes and cunning intents, apparently centered about Cairn but really concerned with someone much more important in the Eastern seas.

Cairn was idly smoking a cheroot on the bridge; he frequently stood loafing here, watching the crowds. Cairn was a man from hell, but did not look it. He was lean and brown and hard, erect and trim in his whites, the four gold stripes of a captain on the arm of his jacket. His hatchet-face was young, almost unlined, and his gray eyes held humorous glints. A man of twenty-five seldom shows the searing scars of hell, except in his actions and reactions.

On either bank were the buildings of Surabaya, half drowned in the luxuriant foliage of Java. The muddy yellow torrent of the Kali Das, the River of Gold, was spotted with native boats. Across the bridge poured an endless tide of humanity; Dutch sepoys, laden coolies, natives in brilliant sarongs, Hindus and Chinese, the throngs starred by unhurried Europeans.

A perspiring Chinese clerk came up to Cairn, spoke him, and handed over a chit. Cairn opened the note and read the brief words:

"Please come to the office. The Ta Ming *is chartered.*
Li Tock Lo."

So the old bumboat was chartered, and he must get on the
job! Cairn smiled. Working for a Chinese shipping firm was
not bad by half, for a man from hell. He liked them, they liked
and trusted him, despite his past.

"Tuan kapitan!" Cairn heard a low, guttural voice, and found a man at his elbow. An old Malay, who spoke very fluent English. "Is there not need for a servant? I am sick at heart for the sea. Once I was a *nakoda*, a ship captain. I am a good steward, cook, quartermaster, servant."

Cairn inspected the man. Why not? In a land of servants, he could well afford a man of his own, and here was one who spoke English. A rather small man, features flat like a dish, a fresh and unhealed knife-scar running across one cheek. Touches of gray at the temples, miserable dirty rags for clothes; neither affluent nor young, this man.

"Your name?"

"Ali, tuan. I can take good care of clothes."

"Your own don't prove it."

"Poverty and illness, tuan, are in the dispensation of Allah."

"You have references?"

"Yes, tuan. I am from Kelantan. I know few people here. But—"

He thrust out a dirty, folded paper. Cairn took it, opened it, and read:

"Ali deserves all trust. I recommend him."

No name was signed; merely a vermilion seal in Chinese. Cairn knew it to be the personal seal of Li Tock Lo, and whistled in surprise. A coincidence, of course. But if shrewd Li Tock Lo recommended anyone, especially a Malay, it meant everything. Chinese and Malays despise each other.

"Very well, you're hired," said Cairn promptly. "We'll talk wages later."

"Agreed, tuan. May Allah requite you!"

CAIRN PRODUCED a key and a banknote. "Here's money; get yourself decent clothes. This is the key of my room at the Hotel Beaulieu, the French one. Go there, pack my things, and await me."

He spoke in Malay, and Ali, showing his black teeth in a grin, departed.

Cairn lit a fresh cheroot and sauntered toward the shipping office. He'd be glad of a servant who spoke English; it would add to his dignity, too. He turned in at Reilly's Bar and had a drink, passed the time of day with the half Irish proprietor, and went his way.

The shipping office was a low, pleasant place where punkas and electric fans stirred the air. Cairn was passed directly into the office of Li Tock Lo, a Straits Chinese of great girth and fat moon-face. Li shook hands cordially, and Cairn dropped into the indicated chair.

"So we're chartered, eh? When do we leave?"

"Stores are going aboard now, Captain. You'll leave in the morning."

Cairn's brows lifted. "But cargo—"

"There is none, on the out trip. A Mynheer Vandunk has chartered the *Ta Ming* for Coomassin in ballast, to return with cargo. He will be here in a few minutes; I wish you to meet him."

Something in the fat Chinaman's manner puzzled Cairn and caught his attention.

"Hm! All right. How about a crew?"

"Vandunk is engaging his own crew and officers, also paying them. You—"

"What the devil!" exclaimed Cairn in astonishment. "But that's not regular!"

"You will sign them on tonight, here at the office," proceeded Li Tock Lo impassively. "Vandunk expects to bring back a valuable cargo and wishes to have men he can trust. It is not regular, but quite natural. I should say that Mynheer Vandunk has influence in the Dutch Colonial Office. He has wealth, and desires more, which Coomassin will give him."

Something in the flat, emotionless voice dinged again at Cairn's attention. There was more than appeared on the surface. He knew this fat yellow man pretty well. It would come out in good time.

"Where's Coomassin?"

"Look in your pilot guide, Captain. The island lies off the Celebes coast; it has no good harbor. I have prepared detailed instructions for your guidance in this respect. It has been semi-independent until last year when the sultan rebelled. The Dutch killed him and took over the island, leaving his daughter on the throne. Most unluckily, bubonic plague broke out. This is now over and ended. A resident and a garrison of sepoys are there. No more trouble. Mynheer Vandunk has a concession covering the island. He is taking with him an English gentleman and his sister who are interested in leasing the rubber plantations from Vandunk. I think that covers the situation, in brief."

"Hm!" Cairn scowled slightly. The scowl made his face harsh, intolerant, cruel. "Concession, eh? What sort?"

"Comprehensive," replied Li Tock Lo. "The island belongs to Mynheer Vandunk."

"By grant of the Dutch government, eh? That means slavery—"

"It is really none of our business," placidly said Li Tock Lo.

"Right; I'm rebuked," and Cairn broke into a laugh. "Look here, Li, I've hired a man. Going to put on a little dog by having my own servant. The fellow said you knew him. He's a Malay named Ali."

"Half the barbarian Malays are named Ali," said Li. "I remember one such man; he is not young, but speaks English. He may be trusted. As a youth, he spent several years in England. His morals are deplorable, but he does not steal."

"Fair enough," and Cairn nodded, "From you, that's a high recommendation."

LI TOCK LO permitted himself a smile. "May I be pardoned for suggesting, Captain, that you do not drink any more today?"

"That's really my own business, Li," said Cairn drily. "I intend to drink, and to drink plenty. I don't get drunk, as you know. I merely blunt memory."

"Absurd. The past is a sharp sword that cannot be blunted." The flat voice was suddenly edged and keen. "I am sending my young relative Erh Tan as supercargo aboard the ship, to which Mynheer Vandunk has agreed. I wish him to be protected. I desire that you do not drink."

"Oh! Fair enough. In that case, it's agreed," said Cairn. "Not until we reach Coomassin, anyhow. I'll take good care of your relative. A young chap, eh?"

Li Tock Lo nodded, produced a fan from his sleeve, and fanned himself gently.

"An estimable youth but inexperienced," he said blandly. "I am trying to teach him that the strongest forces in the world are often those which appear the weakest. A valuable lesson for anyone to know."

Again the indefinite something caught at Cairn. He looked the speaker in the eye.

"Meaning that for me, eh? All right; I get it. What sort of man is Vandunk?"

"I do not know; I have not seen him. His agent arranged everything," Li Tock Lo responded. "His agent is one John Drift, who goes as first officer—"

A buzzer sounded. Li Tock Lo leaned forward and pressed a bell-button on his desk.

"There is Mynheer Vandunk now," he said. "Whether you like him or not, please be very polite; his influence in colonial affairs is large."

The door opened. The fat moon-face of Li Tock Lo expressed surprise, as into the office came a small, brisk man with drooping mustaches and a very red nose.

"Hullo, Li, hullo," he said in English, then blinked at Cairn. "Eh?"

"Why, Mr. Drift!" exclaimed Li Tock Lo. "I expected to see Mynheer Vandunk—"

"Blast it, he went and missed the train at Batavia!" said Drift with evident agitation and a slight cockney accent. "I just 'ad a wire from 'im to see you. He won't get 'ere until morning. That is, the train as gets in about three. He'll go right aboard ship, says 'e."

"So. Mr. Drift, this is Captain Cairn, who commands the ship."

Drift wrung the hand of Cairn and exclaimed cheerfully.

"Glad, sir, perishing glad! Board o' Trade ticket, I take it?"

"Yes," said Cairn. The brisk little man beamed.

"Right, right. First officer in steam—never 'ad my master's examination, blast it! I'll be here at seven tonight to sign on the crew and go aboard, if that suits you, sir".

"Quite," said Cairn. Mr. Drift glanced at his watch.

"I'll 'ave to see Mr. Tracey and 'is sister," he rattled on. "They'll want to get aboard tonight too. At the Netherlands Hotel, they are. The blasted ship 'as no passenger license. I've arranged to sign 'em on as chief stewards and take 'em aboard wi' their luggage late tonight after dinner. I 'opes, sir, it meets with your consent?"

HE PEERED anxiously at Cairn, who nodded. Then he departed. When the door had closed, Li Tock Lo regarded Cairn with a twinkle.

"That man spoke much, and you uttered two words. Hm! I'm sorry not to meet Vandunk. By the way, Captain, I've secured government permission to put a dozen rifles and as many pistols aboard; you know, there's been so much piracy of late along the Celebes coast that the precaution should be observed."

Cairn laughed. "We've nothing worth robbing aboard the *Ta Ming*."

"You may have, returning. And this pirate holds people to ransom. The Dutch and English are both trying to run him down. Singular, they can't even discover much about him!"

"You mean the chap called the Devil's Bosun?" queried Cairn.

"Yes. Said to be a white man, leading natives. Well, let us hope you don't run into him. I should regret having to ransom my young relative, Erh Tan. He will be here this evening at seven, by the way, to be signed on."

"How about stewards?" asked Cairn. "And the black gang?"

"It seems that Vandunk—or his agent—bring a complete crew. Perhaps they, too, are taking no chances on accomplices of the pirates stowing away aboard. It is a wise precaution. Mr. Drift, by the way, is attending to all the ship's papers; through the official assistance extended to Mynheer Vandunk, it is made easy."

A queer business all around, thought Cairn, as he took his departure after all final arrangements. The *Ta Ming* was a small coastwise steamer of no great speed, comfort or ability. She had just got rid of a copra cargo, which increased her usual evil odor, and she was ready to start as soon as stores were in and steam up.

Queer, all of it. Vaguely, indefinitely queer; Li Tock Lo had sensed it without knowing why. Natural enough that a Dutch official would want to put his own crew aboard rather than trust Chinese. The Devil's Bosun was playing the devil with shipping over Borneo way, and often worked by stowing some of his pirates aboard the ship he meant to loot.

Natural enough that an official would be given an island concession. It meant virtual plunder, slavery and death for the unfortunate natives, who did not matter in the least. Particularly if they were Malays and therefore Mohammedan in religion.

Natural enough that an Englishman and his master, probably from Singapore or North Borneo, would want the rubber output. Natural enough that Vandunk should miss his train down from Batavia to Surabaya. And yet all of it, every bit of it, conveyed a queer and indefinite sensation of being a trifle screwy.

SO THINKING, Cairn went back to Reilly's Bar and bought half a case of Irish whiskey to be sent aboard for later consumption. He refused a drink. He was paying Reilly, when he heard a voice behind him.

"Bill, if that isn't Mark Hudson, I'm a liar! It's Hudson, I tell you! Hey, Mark! Mark!"

Cairn paid no attention. A hand caught his arm. He turned, to see two men staring at him. He knew them both instantly; but his look of surprised interrogation was perfectly assumed.

"I beg your pardon," said one of the two, a bit confused by that straight, blank look. "But aren't you Mark Hudson? You must be—you remember me—we were both in your class at Annapolis—"

Cairn's brows lifted. "Sorry," he said, with a deliberate English accent on the word. "Mistake, no doubt. My name is Cairn."

"Here's your change, Cap'n Cairn," broke in Reilly, handing

over money. Cairn took it, nodded, and walked out, leaving the two Americans looking after him. They turned to Reilly and overwhelmed the latter with questions.

"No manner of use, gents," said Reilly. "I've knowed him a couple o' year. Master in steam he is—Cap'n Cairn. Where from? Lor' bless you! Liverpool Irish as ever was. Told me so hisself. What'll it be, gents?"

The two shook their heads at each other. A mistake, of course; Mark Hudson had been drowned the night before the court-martial. Had tried to escape and had been drowned. An old Annapolis custom. Damned good thing, too; saved all hands from disgrace. Drunken robbery, a woman tangled up in it—yes, a damned good thing. Men who made mistakes of that sort had no business in the navy.

But Cairn, cursing under his breath, walked home to his French hotel with eyes so bitter and hard that men who met him, turned sharply away. He needed a drink now, wanted a dozen drinks, a whole bottle. Why the devil had he promised not to take a drink until he reached Coomassin? Now was when he needed it most.

He found Ali in his room, quietly packing his things. The dish-faced little old Malay now wore a fresh sarong and jacket. His teeth were quite black from chewing betel-paste, Cairn observed.

"Well, Ali! We're going to Coomassin. Know where that is?"

"No, tuan kapitan. I never heard of it."

"So much the better. Neither did I. You're free until seven tonight."

"If the tuan permits, I will stay here."

"Suit yourself. Lay out a fresh suit for me." Cairn departed to his bath. Later, he found his clothes ready, and flung a laughing question at Ali. "Where'd you learn so much about getting clothes ready?"

"By having servants of my own, tuan," said Ali. Cairn did not press the topic, from a feeling of delicacy.

A S H E had not eaten since morning, he was ready for a very early dinner—he had to be at the office by seven. He left everything packed, gave Ali money and orders to be there with his bags at the appointed time, and swung out of the little hotel.

What was the name of those English people? Tracey, yes, and at the Netherlands. Cairn went straight there, being curious. Woman aboard, eh? Not so good. Still, these stiff Englishwomen didn't matter; they were sexless creatures, as a rule. Not like blooming, rosy Eurasian girls.

Cairn caught sight of them talking with Mr. Drift. He dropped into a chair, held up a newspaper, and kept an eye on them. At first he was staggered. Tracey was a young fellow, blond and eager, but far gone in liquor; nearly drunk, in fact. The sister was slim and cool, lovely as a flower unfolding. Cairn regarded her sourly, appraising her with jaundiced eye. Too damned cool altogether, too capable, bound by restraint and icy convention. Bah!

Mr. Drift went off with the young fellow, toward the bar. Cairn caught a flash of emotion in the girl's face as she looked after them—anxiety, even fear, widening the lovely blue eyes. He let the newspaper fall. She felt his gaze and her eyes touched on him for an instant, then drifted away. She rose and departed.

With a scornful grunt, Cairn strode off to get his dinner.

"I bet the Dutchman trims those two Britishers," he reflected. "Rubber, eh? And she tags along to keep the young fool sober—which she doesn't do. Bah! Bet she gets a few healthy shocks at Coomassin, or before. Do her good."

Dinner over, with time to spare, Captain Cairn drifted back to Reilly's Bar in order to meet a Scotch tramp skipper whom he wanted to see. He did not find his man, but two officers of a Burns-Philp boat were standing at the bar after many drinks, and one of them uttered the name of Coomassin.

"Sultan of Coomassin's daughter—aye, that's who she is," said one, handing over a photograph. "I hear she's running the bloody outfit now. Did you ever see the likes? My good gosh, what a woman! What a woman!"

"Aye, she's likely enough," said the other, with a catch in his voice.

Cairn came up beside them and looked. A pulse leaped in him at sight of the pictured face. Sultan's daughter? Nonsense! Pure Caucasian, and ineffably lovely; a face to take away the breath of a man, eyes to hold his heart—one of those chance pictures where the eyes look out and pierce.

"Hi, there! Who are you, horning in?" With an oath, the two Aussies swung angrily around. Cairn laughed, reached forward, and took the picture. A fist swung into his midriff.

His fists struck out, lightly it seemed. A blow smashed him squarely in the eye; those two could fight. Glasses shivered, Reilly shrieked for help. One of the two went staggering down the length of the bar. The other spun around and was knocked over a table, and went crashing down with it.

Cairn, still laughing, strode out. In the street, he paused to look again at the picture. Head and shoulders, no more. An almost Grecian face, smiling a little, so unutterably perfect and adorable that his pounding heart stood still.

"Sultan's daughter, hell!" said Cairn, as he thrust it safely away. "There, by God, is a woman—a real woman, not an iceberg! Now I know why I'm going to Coomassin."

HE WALKED into the shipping office at seven o'clock with one eye puffed and blackening. The brisk Mr. Drift was there, and so were the other officers. Lochaber, a portly Scotch engineer, and his assistant who had Chinese blood. Andrews, second officer; a dark, taciturn man with cruel devils in his black eyes and an ugly twist to his lips. A powerful fellow, Andrews. Chinese steward, halfbreed quartermasters; black gang, deck hands, cook and helper—all halfbreeds or Malays or Chinese. Not a Dutchman in the lot.

And this was the queerest thing of all, thought Cairn.

Evidently Erh Tan thought the same thing, and the other

clerks; Li Tock Lo was not here. Erh Tan was a plump young man, small, clad in black jacket and skirt of beautiful silk brocade; his features were exquisitely carven, like old ivory. His eyes flitted in surprise and wonder over the assembled men. He turned, caught the gaze of Cairn, and smiled slightly.

Cairn liked him. He did not like this crew. None was drunk; and this was a strange thing, also. He had a word with Lochaber, the chief engineer. An unpleasant fat rascal of perhaps fifty, loose-lipped and heavy-jowled, with an odor about him. Over the room hung the same odor. Cairn had sharp nostrils, and sniffed at it with a frown. He touched Erh Tan on the elbow and met the slitted eyes.

"What is it I smell?" he said under his breath. "What's this odor?"

"Chandu," muttered the yellow man.

Opium, eh? The whole lot of them. That looked queer, too.

Cairn wondered what was the matter with him, that he should have this strange feeling about the whole business. Perhaps, meeting those two Americans and being recognized? No, not that.

The only natural touch to the affair was that of the Tracey girl; and Cairn grunted again at thought of her. The picture in his pocket—well, it might be a mistake. Those two Australians might have lied about it. No telling.

The comprador wakened him from his musing. All ready to go aboard; the boats were waiting.

A silent lot. No jokes, no stories, no talking. Less and less did Cairn like his outfit, but they were signed on now; no backing down. He found himself curious to see Vandunk. Mr. Drift stuck close to his side, chattering and rattling away with eternal nervous energy. Nervous? By God, that might be it! The brisk little devil was nervous. What about? Then Mr. Drift departed to seek the passengers.

Questions died. The river, the harbor, the glinting lights, the boats awaiting them, the men piling in with their duffel-bags.

Cairn wanted another look at the photograph in his pocket, and wanted it badly.

There was the old scow now, with sampans and boats around her, stores going in, stevedores at work. Li Tock Lo attended to everything. Now Cairn was to take over—a queer sea-going, this! But, with the decking under his feet, he became a different man, alert and alive, all dreams departed, pictures forgotten.

Mr. Drift was to come aboard an hour later with the Traceys.

CAIRN PITCHED into details, getting the new crowd shaken down and everything shipshape. He stole time off for a visit to his cabin, under the bridge. There he emptied his pockets, glanced at the photograph, and put it down with a smile. Ali was stowing away his things, quietly efficient. Cairn saw the Irish whiskey and locked it into his private cupboard, and went back on deck.

There he reached for his pipe, found it forgotten, and returned to his cabin. As he stepped in, he caught sight of Ali, holding the picture of the girl, staring at it. The Malay whipped around, startled agitation in his scarred face.

"Hello!" exclaimed Cairn. "Do you know the lady, Ali?"

"No, tuan," humbly replied the little brown man. "But her face is one in which there is no luck." And so saying, Ali left the cabin.

No luck? Cairn looked at the picture, met the wide, lovely eyes, and thrilled to them anew. He understood what Ali had meant. This girl was too exquisite, too perfect a thing, to have any great luck. She would be looted, plundered, used, a tool in the rapacious hands of conquerors.

"Probably she's Eurasian," thought Cairn. "A sultana in Coomassin, but in any white man's town a despised outcast. Well, by heaven—"

He checked his thoughts, shoved the picture into a drawer, and went back on deck. He came slap on Mr. Andrews, the dark second officer, standing on the bridge in talk with two of the men from forward—in talk and laughter, as though some smutty jest had just been passed. Cairn halted.

"I thought you had charge of stowing those stores, Mr. Andrews?" he said. "You men, go below. Don't come on the bridge again except on duty."

"What the hell!" Andrews swung around. "Don't be so high-faluting on this old bumboat. You ain't going to run this hooker navy style—"

Cairn hit him twice, and hard, and carefully. Not at all like a gentleman, but like a man who meant to win his fight then and there. The two brown men disappeared like shadows. Mr. Andrews clamped both hands over his belly and leaned back against the bridge-house in agony, his dark eyes rolling.

"Don't make mistakes again," said Cairn, his voice cold and cruel. "I'm running this hooker any style I damned please. You're taking orders, not giving them. Wipe that look off your face and get to work, or I'll murder you."

Murder lay in the eyes of Andrew's, but it was downed by suffering; he was all but paralyzed. He gasped out something and staggered away. Cairn went into the wheel house, examined his fine black eye, and fell to work with charts and pilot guide.

MR. DRIFT brought the Traceys aboard. Cairn met them at the rail and was formally introduced. Tracey was pleasantly drunk and affable. He shook hands and hurried off with Mr. Drift to look after the mountains of luggage streaming aboard. Miss Tracey moved aside with Cairn and spoke in a low, controlled voice.

"You were sitting in the hotel this evening, watching us. But you did not have that mouser at the time."

Cairn chuckled. "Right. It's a beautiful shiner, eh? Yes, I wanted to see what our passengers looked like. What do you think of the ship?"

"She's pretty dreadful," said Miss Tracey, with the usual English habit of speaking one's mind. "I don't understand why you should have such a ship."

"Eh? Oh, is that base flattery? You don't know the truth. I'm lucky to have any ship at all, much less the *Ta Ming*. The 'Great Enlightened' is one translation of the words. I think we'll need a lot of enlightenment this voyage."

"I think so, too," she answered calmly. "What is Mr. Vandunk like?"

"Eh? But you know him—"

"We know only his agent, Mr. Drift."

"That's queer. Well, I don't know Vandunk either. He'll be aboard sometime in the morning, before we sail. May I show you your cabins?"

He did so, called the Chinese steward, and put him at the lady's disposition. Then he bade his guests good night and got Mr. Drift to work. And Mr. Drift could work; he immediately relieved Cairn of all details in an admirably brisk manner.

It was after three in the morning when a launch brought Mynheer Vandunk aboard. Cairn, who had expected a brawny Hollander, was disappointed. The man who came over the rail was rather small, and enveloped in coat and shawl against the river mist, until only a pair of bright little eyes were visible. His handshake was limp.

"Glad to meet you, Captain," he said in English. "I must get to my cabin and go over matters with Mr. Drift, if you'll allow. The moment we start I'll be awfully sick. I get seasick with the first wave. I just can't help it. I'll be sick for days and days. That's why I can't abide the sea, just can't abide it. Good morning."

So this was Mynheer Vandunk! Cairn looked reflectively after him, then turned as a limp, senseless figure was lifted on deck under Mr. Drift's direction.

"Who the devil's this?" Cairn demanded. The first officer winked.

"Mynheer Vandunk's servant, sir—unfortunately, he's a bit addicted to the poppy. A fine fellow in his right senses. I'll have him placed in Mynheer Vandunk's cabin; the master likes to have him close at hand."

Cairn shrugged and sought the bridge. "Can't abide the sea!" Now that was a strange expression for any Dutchman to use, even if the speaker had been educated in England or were half English. And it seemed odd that the Traceys should be taking a long trip with investment possibilities ahead, yet did not know Vandunk. Of course it was customary to deal through agents—and yet it seemed odd.

"Something queer back of it all," Cairn told himself. "The Traceys aren't crooked. The young fellow's a fool for liquor, the girl's got the brains of the two. Still, there's something that doesn't show on the surface. I can feel it. So could Li Tock Lo. Something screwy."

Cairn turned to the instructions given him by Li Tock Lo. These merely concerned the Coomassin anchorage, which was exposed and unsafe. In case weather came up while Cairn was awaiting the return cargo, he was to run the ship into the river-mouth on the Celebes mainland, opposite the island.

So, with the turn of the tide, the *Ta Ming* put out to sea, with ballast of sharp death and subtle destiny.

CHAPTER II

"STRANGE! HE doesn't look a bit like his picture," said Stella Tracey. Her brother turned to her in surprise. "Where'd you see his picture?"

"In Surabaya. I showed it to you, but you'd been drinking and paid no heed. It was in that government handbook we looked over; it told how he meant to turn Coomassin into a model district. He has full powers there, you know."

The speakers sat overlooking the after well deck. Cairn had come aft for a look around, before going to the bridge. Stella Tracey had a book in her lap. Her brother was mouthing a pipe, with moody, frowning air.

"Why did Vandunk send for you and not me?" he demanded irritably.

"Because I'm handling the business end, naturally."

Cairn hesitated. So Vandunk didn't look like his pictures, eh? Interesting if true; but few people do look like their pictures.

It was early afternoon. Rijstaafel, the enormous noonday meal of Java, was over. Cairn had everything running smoothly; the ship was pounding through a level, calm sea that was hardly ruffled by a breeze.

"Good afternoon!" Cairn approached the two. "Everything all right?"

"Oh, quite, thanks," said Tracey. "Sit down, do—take my chair."

"Can't possibly, to my regret," said Cairn. "I'm due on the bridge. By the way, if either of you care to come up there at any time, barge ahead."

Stella Tracey looked up at him, a peculiarly frank and level look.

"Thanks. If you'll not sit down, I may be up presently. I'd like a word with you when you've time."

"At your service," replied Cairn. "But I must run now. Come when you like."

He touched his cap and went up the after bridge ladder. Andrews, who was on duty, met him with a nod that betrayed no rancor.

"The steward was just here, sir, looking for you. Mynheer Vandunk would like a word with you when you've time to step down."

"Right," said Cairn, and lit his pipe. The quartermaster at the wheel saluted him. A bony-faced brown man, a halfbreed of sorts on a Malay base. A good seaman.

"I'm sorry about last night, sir," Andrews said unexpectedly.

Cairn laughed. "Forget it, if you can also forget what caused it. How on earth did you and Mr. Drift happen to be hired by a Dutchman?"

"Can't say for Mr. Drift, sir. For myself, I was out of a berth and got this one through knowing the Celebes coast a bit. And a clean ticket."

"Lucky man," Cairn commented drily.

FIVE MINUTES later, he saw Stella Tracey coming to the bridge. He was surprised by her speedy appearance, and surprised again when she halted at the leeward rail, as though to speak beyond hearing of anyone else. This, it proved, was her intent.

"Did anything queer or extraordinary take place last night, Captain Cairn?"

"Not to my knowledge." Cairn met her flashing blue eyes. "Why?"

"No one fell overboard?"

Cairn laughed. "I hope not! No, certainly not. Please tell me why."

"Then I must have been wrong." She hesitated, and continued. "You see, before daylight I was awakened. At first I thought by the movement of the ship at sea; but I heard voices next door. My cabin is next that of Mynheer Vandunk; next me, and farther aft, is that of my brother. The noise came from Vandunk's cabin. My port was open, and so, I imagine, was his."

Cairn nodded. "What sort of noise?"

"Excited voices. I could hear nothing of what was said; the tone was excited. I went to close my port. As I did so, I saw something fall. It was as though a man had jumped from the port next door. A voice said, 'He's gone.' That was all. I could not swear to it, mind. I was sleepy at the time. The whole thing must have been a mental error on my part."

"Perhaps; perhaps not," said Cairn. "It's good of you to have told me this, Miss Tracey. I'll look into it, without mentioning you. There are all sorts of queer goings-on when a ship leaves port, so don't be uneasy."

She laughed lightly. "Oh, I'm not! And I don't think your

ship is half so bad as I did last night, really. By the way, have
you ever been at Coomassin?"

"Never. Nor you?"

"No. My brother was there three or four years ago, when he
first came out. He liked the place, and quite lost his heart to
the sultan's daughter. I understand she's grown up now, and has
become the sultana. Odd for a white girl, eh?"

Cairn's heart skipped a beat.

"White girl? But you said, the sultan's daughter—"

"Yes indeed. I believe she was the child of some trader who
had no other family, and the sultan adopted her. Romantic,
what?"

Cairn nodded. "I suppose so. If true. In these waters, romance
usually turns out to be pretty sordid stuff that won't bear looking
into. A white girl—and a sultana? I'll believe that when I see
it."

She departed in frigid disapproval. Cairn cursed himself;
what had impelled him to such savage words? In no pleasant
mood, he sought the cabin of Vandunk, and at his knock was
told to enter.

HE FOUND Vandunk seated before a table littered with
papers from an open portfolio. Cairn's impression was one of
astonishment. The man was small, rotund, beaming with merriment; little shoe-button eyes danced, his thick lips curved.
He had a heavy cleft chin and high forehead, and was health-
ily bronzed. But there was no humor in his mirth. It was like
a mask.

"Well, well, Captain! Seasick, says I; and here you find me
hard at work. Even keel and no swell, eh? Well, I'll no doubt
be sick enough tonight. Sit down, sir. A cheroot? Prime stuff,
you'll find 'em."

Cairn accepted a whitish cheroot of fine tobacco, and seated
himself. The little shoe-button eyes darted over him in appraisal.

"You speak English well," said Cairn.

"And why not? First twenty years of my life were spent in Norfolk, Cap'n. All well aboard?"

"Well enough," said Cairn, and lit his cheroot. "Who fell out of your port last night?"

He meant to catch Vandunk off guard; and did it. For a moment the man seemed to freeze in every line of his rotund face. But the black little eyes dilated until the whites showed clear around the pupils, and the thick lips hardened, and the limp hand on the desk made a jerky movement—as though to dive for a weapon. Then it stopped.

"That's what I called you down about, Cap'n," Vandunk said slowly. "My servant, poor devil! Out of his head with opium and bhang. He kicked up a bit of a row early this morning. You know how these Malays are, and the queer insanity that comes upon 'em at times, like running amok? This is the other kind, congenital. The poor devil was out of the port before I knew it, and gone."

Cairn nodded silently. He remembered the limp figure that had come aboard.

"I don't suppose you'll have to enter it in the log?" asked Vandunk.

"Not unless you want it entered. It's none of my affair."

Vandunk drew a deep breath, as of relief. "Right you are, Cap'n. You'll not lose by it, I promise you. I take it you know what's ahead of us?"

"Vaguely. No details."

Vandunk took a cheroot and bit at it, and relaxed in his seat.

"I'm to take over Coomassin for the government. I want to ship out a good deal of stuff at once; I'll have a cargo, or part of one, for you within a week, I hope. It may go to Sarawak or Macassar. We'll see about that. But there may be a bit of trouble. Two of our men, Mr. Andrews and Mr. Lochaber, were at the island at the time of the revolt and in fact were in the service of the sultan. They were, if I may so phrase it, agents of ours and in consequence the natives may remember the fact. They'll have to be careful about going ashore and so on. Don't give them any shore leave."

"I see," said Cairn. "To put it bluntly, I presume they're considered as traitors."

"That's it," and Vandunk gave him a in narrow glance. "You don't know the island?"

"Never heard of it before yesterday."

"Very well." Vandunk gestured to the litter of papers. "I've everything here to put me in full authority. Your ship's under charter to me. You take orders only from me. Is that understood?"

"Naturally," said Cairn.

"Then we understand each other," Vandunk said, and shook hands in dismissal. "I'll be a sick man tonight, I fear; looks like wind in the north. Well, good luck to you!"

CAIRN SOUGHT his own cabin, with mixed feelings. Looks like wind in the north, eh? This man spoke like a seaman. He was a Dutch colonial official, and unlike any of the ilk Cairn had ever met or seen. Yet a keen eye cast at those papers on the table had shown him that they were official papers. Yes, Vandunk was simply a queer sort of man, a square peg in a round hole as it were.

Ali was straightening up the cabin. He had a bandage about his face, and complained that the knife-wound over his cheek was swollen and painful. Cairn made him take off the bandage. The wound looked perfectly all right, but Cairn dosed it with iodine none the less and Ali replaced the bandage. This was just being finished when a knock sounded at the door, then Mr. Drift stuck his head in. His eyes rolled.

"Cap'n! Cap'n!" he said sharply. "Oh, this is terrible, awful! Come along, sir. Mr. Lochaber's cabin—the chief's dead, sir."

Cairn followed him on the jump. Lochaber's cabin was just across the passage. Cairn entered behind the first officer, and

Mr. Drift pointed. On the floor lay the fat old chief, dead, and dreadfully dead. He had been stabbed twice.

With shaking fingers, Mr. Drift laid bare the wounds. They were neat and clean. No blood at all. Cairn knelt, then glanced up. Erh Tan stood in the open doorway, and now came forward. The plump young Chinese showed no agitation, but looked down at the dead man and the exposed wounds. His voice came calmly, clearly.

"Strange! A kris *melala* did this work."

"What's that?" snapped Cairn. "What do you mean?"

"Look at the wounds, Captain," the young Chinese said. "Each shows very clearly that it was done by a knife with a raised ridge down the center. This could only be a certain form of kris used by Malays of the highest rank."

Mr. Drift felt the hands of the dead man.

"Stiff," he muttered in agitation. "He didn't show up at noon mess—that's why I looked in on him, and found him. Must have been done when he went off watch at eight bells, noon. As soon as he came into his cabin. Captain Cairn, what can we do about this murder?"

"Go take the deck and send Mr. Andrews here," said Cairn, rising. "Erh Tan, will you find the steward?"

Cairn was alone with the dead man. He looked about; the cabin showed nothing of the least interest. A duffel-bag, half-emptied, a half filled locker, afforded no help. Then Mr. Andrews came in, and his dark features were gray.

"Poor old devil!" he exclaimed. "Poor Tom Lochabe—"

"Get to work," said Cairn. "You and me both. Don't waste words; there's somebody aboard who murdered him. Why? We'll go through every cabin and every man until we find the weapon that did it. A kris with a ridge down the blade."

Andrews stared at him, and fright shook the dark man.

"A kris—ridged! A sultan's kris—no, no!" cried Andrews. "I tell you, it can't be, it can't! Not that, Cap'n. You don't know about it, but—"

"What's got into you?" snapped Cairn angrily. "You and the chief are old friends. Buck up! We'll find the murdering devil who did this. Go through every native aboard. Oh, there's the steward—come along! Start with him. Take him for'ard and I'll be along as soon as I've spoken with the assistant engineer."

Andrews gripped the yellow steward and they disappeared, leaving a wake of oaths and protesting squeaks.

CAIRN LOOKED around the cabin once more, went to the half-open bag, and dumped it. Shoes fell out, a Bible, a tattered copy of Burns' poems, half a dozen knick-knacks, and two new Webley automatics with a box of cartridges. Incredulous, Cairn picked them up, examined them. Never fired, apparently, but cleaned of all grease. Service pistols, new, fresh, unscratched, empty. And cartridges for them. Where would a fat old engineer get such things—in Java? What would he want with them?

Cairn took them to his own cabin, locked them away, and sought the engine-room. The assistant, an empty-eyed fellow half Dutch and half native, gawked and blinked and knew nothing. Mynheer Lochaber had gone off watch. Trouble with anyone? Enemies? Not at all. The black gang all liked the old chief.

Cairn learned nothing. He joined Andrews forward, where the crew were mustered. The outcome was very curious. The whereabouts of every man was definitely shown, at the change of watches. Even Ali, the Malay, had been lending the steward a hand at the mess table. A search of the men's quarters showed no weapon of any kind.

Andrews resumed his watch. Cairn went to the bridge and found three men in the pilot-house; Andrews, the quartermaster and Mynheer Vandunk. The latter was in a white fury. Cairn heard him cursing, but he checked himself as Cairn appeared. His little eyes were like blazing coals.

"Who did this murder, Cap'n?" he shot out.

"Don't ask me," said Cairn wearily. "Every man for'ard has an alibi. Someone aft did it—or these men are good liars."

"None of my men did it!" exclaimed Vandunk vehemently. His voice was deep, authoritative, charged with power. "Lochaber was a favorite with the men. I've looked into the record of every man aboard. Perhaps you did it yourself?"

"Are you drunk?" Cairn surveyed him with quick appraisal.

"I beg your pardon," said Vandunk. "I'm a bit worked up— Lochaber was an old friend. I'm terribly agitated. Oh, my stomach! I must get back to my cabin. I can't stand the motion up here on the bridge—"

He departed hastily. Andrews watched Cairn with smoldering gaze, and spoke.

"I think he's had a bit to drink, sir. Most upset, he was. I don't mind saying it got me a bit, too. The chief and I have been places together."

"So Vandunk told me," Cairn said drily. "Enter it up in the log. We'll have the burial at sunset."

To the surprise of Cairn, young Tracey eagerly volunteered to act as assistant engineer, the half-blood assistant becoming chief. Tracey knew engines, looked on it as a distinct lark, and threw himself into the job with a will.

Mr. Drift and Cairn searched everything aft, from captain's cabin to cook's galley, but no kris or knife with a ridged blade was turned up. The rifles and pistols that had been put aboard, Cairn kept under lock and key; he said nothing of the two new Webleys reposing in his private locker.

NEXT MORNING, feeling the swell of the Straits of Macassar, the *Ta Ming* was wallowing through a heavy quartering sea. Both the Traceys were seasick and, the steward being busy, Ali took his place at breakfast. Mr. Drift and Cairn were at the table together, then the chief officer departed and Andrews took his place, with a glance at the little brown man, whose face was still bandaged.

"Can't get it out of my head that I've seen you before, Ali," said Andrews. "Macassar, perhaps? Or aboard some craft?"

"No, tuan," Ali responded in his humble way. "If I had ever seen the tuan before, I would not forget him. Ya Allah! The slave does not forget the great ones whom he has served."

"Huh! I'll remember sooner or later," said Andrews. "Well, Cap'n, Mr. Tracey is a bit of all right. Sick as a dog, but sticking to his job. We'll manage."

Cairn happened to look up, caught a glance that Ali threw at the second mate, and was momentarily startled. The gleam and glitter in Ali's eyes, the flashing scorn and even hatred—no, he must have misread the look. It was gone instantly. Perhaps Ali resented having to act as steward, for some of these Malays were devilish touchy.

Later, Cairn looked up Erh Tan and found the plump young fellow terribly gripped by seasickness. The ship was rolling like a pig. Toward noon, Cairn went to the bridge, and while awaiting Mr. Drift to take the noon sights, fell into talk with Andrews. He had put the second officer down as a thorough bad one, but he got a bit of a surprise.

"Vandunk tells me you've been at Coomassin. I've heard stories about the sultan there having an adopted daughter, a white girl. Any truth in the yarn?"

"Yes," said Andrews, and his hard face softened. "Amina, her name was. The most beautiful creature ever lived, Cap'n; a living angel, that girl was. I reckon she never had a bad thought, even—think me a damn fool, I s'pose?"

"No," said Cairn softly. "Tell me more about her."

"Ain't much to tell. She was a trader's daughter. The old sultan adopted her. She's got his throne now. I s'pose the Dutch will marry her off to some official and make sure of Coomassin. Everybody loved her—in a right way, mind you. Why, you take even me! I'd ha' gone into hell for her. And old Lochaber, who had four native women then, he'd get mighty ashamed if Amina even looked his way. Well, some women are like that. Have a queer effect on you."

Mr. Drift appeared with his instruments, and the conversation ended.

The noon meal was a sea snack and no mistake, with everything rolling great guns and the Chinese steward hard put to it at times to keep right side up. Stella Tracey showed up, white but brave, to cope with tea and toast.

The steward set a huge plate of curry before Cairn, especially decorated for him by the cook—shrimp, fish, meat, rice, arranged in fantastic manner. There was some laughter, Mr. Drift complaining loudly that nobody bothered to fix *his* plate navy style. Cairn attacked the dish with a will, and was part way through it when Ali appeared suddenly.

"Tuan kapitan! Mr. Ehr Tan wants you at once. He says he is dying and must see you—"

"Dying?" Cairn started up. "What's happened?"

"Nothing, tuan. He is seasick."

Cairn broke into a laugh. "All right, I'll come along and reassure him. Cover my plate and keep it warm, steward."

HE STARTED for Erh Tan's cabin, only to find Ali suddenly gripping his arm, looking into his face with blazing eyes.

"It was a lie, tuan. Go quickly, quickly! Your own cabin. Be sick. I came into the galley and saw the cook put a white powder into your curry. Poison. Ya Allah! There is no time to lose."

Poison—it was incredible! But the air, the suddenly vigorous tone of Ali, smashed the fact home. White powder? It might be some mistake or it might not.

Cairn went for his cabin with a rush. He got rid of his meal; then, white and shaken, he questioned Ali. The Malay really knew nothing, had merely seen the cook dosing the plate of curry with a white powder, and had jumped to conclusions. Cairn was tempted to anger, but repressed the feeling; such loyalty was too rare to be jeopardized.

He went back to the mess cabin and found only Miss Tracey there, lingering over her tea. Cairn told the steward to bring the cook at once.

The cook arrived. He was a lean, pockmarked fellow, with Malay features and oblique Chinese eyes. Cairn addressed him in English.

"The curry you made for me is excellent. I desire to compliment you. Unfortunately, my hunger does not permit me to eat so large an amount, therefore, as a mark of my favor, I desire you to finish the plate. Give it to him, steward."

The cook took the plate, and his face assumed a grayish look.

"Captain, no can do," he said in a thin voice. "Seasick. Velly sick. No can eat; all come topside quick. Velly solly."

Cairn smiled grimly. "Eat it, or I'll call two men to hold you and have it crammed down your throat. Eat it!"

"Why, Captain Cairn!" exclaimed the girl quickly. "You can see he's desperately ill—he can't possibly eat that curry! The very sight of it—"

The cook's eyes darted about. Then, like a flash, he was at the nearest port. With one hand he unscrewed it, and before Cairn could grab him, he had the thick glass open—and the plate went flying out. Then he crumpled in Cairn's hands, and made no resistance.

"Get the off watch quartermaster and two men," snapped Cairn at the steward.

Five minutes later, the cook was taken away to be laid in irons, and Cairn went to the galley. Miss Tracey, wondering and a little angry because he ignored her, followed him. In the galley, Cairn turned on her.

"This is a case of poisoning, since you've got to know. Now keep quiet."

Presently he had what he sought; a folded paper such as chemists use, crumpled in one corner. Cairn opened it up. A few white grains of powder showed. He tasted them and made a wry grimace. Already he knew that the warning had come barely in time; a feeling of constriction was creeping through arms and legs, and his heart was pounding.

"Strychnine," he said curtly. "Miss Tracey, will you be good enough to find Mr. Drift—get him to my cabin at once. I didn't get enough of it to kill, but I may be knocked out for a bit. Hurry."

Once in his own cabin, he got into pajamas, took out one of the Webleys, loaded it, and took it to bed with him. Ali did not appear. When Mr. Drift showed up, Cairn regarded him grimly.

"Take charge. Sweat that cook; try and make him talk. I got rid of the poison in time, but the paralysis has got me. I'll be an hour or two before I can do anything. Heart's going hard."

Mr. Drift disappeared briskly. Then Cairn found Stella Tracey sitting beside him. Cool, capable, she silenced his protests.

"I've talked with Ali. Now keep quiet, Cap'n. Let me make things easy for you; best to let it wear off. I'm not a bad nurse, really."

CAIRN DRIFTED. He would be all right later, and knew it; but the constriction was hard to bear. Her deft ministrations, her tenderness, astonished and softened him. She was a very beautiful woman, was Stella Tracey.

His brain was clear enough on certain subjects, but he could talk only with difficulty. She was making him drink quantities of hot black coffee all the time. She did the talking herself; told him a lot about herself, even about the man over in Kedah, in the civil service, to whom she was engaged. She talked rapidly, trying to keep his mind occupied. Why anyone would try to poison the captain of the *Ta Ming* was a mystery, and she said so.

"More'n one mystery here," mumbled Cairn. "All this crowd aboard speaks English. Why? Most of the men, too. All picked men. Vandunk picked the cook."

"Well, don't think about it," she said. "Any signs of convulsions?"

"Nope. Just the first stage; nothing worse ahead," and Cairn laughed. "Saw a chap die of strychnine once, and it's damned unpleasant. Sorry—my rudeness. You're an angel."

"Oh, you're not a bad sort!" she replied brightly. "Tell me something—I saw this on the shelf yonder," and she held up the photograph of Amina. "A friend of yours? I'm interested, because I never saw a more lovely face in all my life. Who is she, if I may ask?"

"Not sure myself," Cairn said. "Took it away from a couple of chaps—in Reilly's Bar, in Surabaya. They said it was Amina, the Coomassin girl we were talking about—the other day. Not sure—"

Presently Erh Tan appeared in the doorway. He stayed only a moment, inquired very politely after Cairn, and went his way.

Ali showed up. His bandage was gone now, and Cairn noted that the wound on his cheek was healing well. He squatted in one corner, in the respectful style of Malays, and said little.

Cairn was beginning to feel more like himself; the cold sweat was passing, and the constriction, and the slight paralysis was also departing. Then, suddenly, Mr. Drift walked in and shut the door. He removed his cap, and wiped his forehead.

"Blast it! I've had one hell of a time—excuse me, miss. Terrible, Cap'n, but there warn't no 'elp for it. I fair 'ad to shoot the blighter. Come at me with a knife, he did. Pulled it out of behind his neck."

Cairn came to one elbow. "Who the devil are you talking about?"

"That ruddy cook, sir." The brisk Mr. Drift was agitated and earnest. "I was a-hauling of 'im over the coals when he done it. Lucky I 'ad my gun at hand, and let 'im have it. But it fair broke me up; put me all in a shake."

"Did you get any information out of him?" demanded Cairn. "Any reason for having poisoned me?"

"Not a smell, sir. It was me what signed 'im on, too; best of credentials and references. He'd been assistant cook in one o' them Bombay boats." Mr. Drift wiped his brow again. "I've put the steward on to the galley job, sir, and it struck me that if this here Malay of yours would act as steward—"

"That's for him to say. What about it, Ali?"

ALI, SQUATTING in the corner, regarded them with a grim smile, an ironic smile, a smile proud and scornful at once. Then it was gone.

"What else can I do?" he said with a shrug. "Allah gives one man the power to order, another the faculty of obedience. I serve you, tuan."

"Good. Then that's arranged," said Mr. Drift with relief. "Now I'll 'ave to look up Mr. Andrews, blast him! He should be on the bridge, but he ain't. I'll just take a look in his cabin. Feeling better, sir?"

"Quite," Cairn rejoined. "I'm pretty much myself."

Mr. Drift departed briskly. Cairn looked at the little brown man.

"Ali, I'm in your debt; I don't forget debts. Thanks to you, I'm alive. And thanks to Miss Tracey, here, I'm quite all right again. By the way, Ali, have you any idea why that rascal wanted to kill me?"

"None, tuan," returned the Malay, rearranging his sarong as he squatted. "But he would certainly have talked, had he lived to talk."

"What do you mean by that?" demanded Stella Tracey suddenly, in Malay. "What is in your mind? You are no man of low caste; you are a raja at least, a man of some rank. What do your words mean?"

Ali looked blank. "Once I was a raja, yes; now I am a servant, by the will of Allah. Nothing was in my mind. The words were idle."

The door burst open.

"My God!" Mr. Drift came stumbling into the room, catching at the door as the ship rolled. He was livid, his eyes bulging. "My God! Poor Andrews has got it—just like the chief—laying in 'is cabin all blood, and dead, stone dead. Just like the chief, sir—stabbed twice—"

Cairn was out of bed, and caught up the pistol as his feet touched the floor.

CHAPTER III

DEATH HOVERED above the *Ta Ming* as she ploughed the eastern seas, and not death alone, but murder. It filled her like a living presence. Murder, stark and terrible in the sunlight, dread and whispering under the stars.

The utterly baffling mystery of it was horrible. Officers and men—all hands were jerky, eyes darting over shoulders, dark places shunned, cabin doors locked and ports screwed shut. A stiff sea was running, so that the clumsy little hooker kept rolling savagely, as though dodging the finger of death that reached into her vitals.

A couple of days put Cairn on his feet, as well as ever in body, but mentally aghast before the undeniable facts that faced him. Time had elapsed, giving him full opportunity to run down every clue and pin the murder upon the right man—and it was impossible. The murderer was by far too clever.

Andrews had not been long dead when Mr. Drift found him; but the time of his death could not be approximated. He, like Lochaber, had been stabbed twice by a kris with ridged blade. The same weapon, its mark clearly defined.

"I've run down nothing," said Cairn to Stella Tracey. She had come up to the bridge during his afternoon watch. They stood at the lee rail together, beyond hearing of the quartermaster in the house.

"About three persons I'm absolutely sure. One's the cook, because he had just been shot. You and I were together in my cabin. Everybody else aboard is covered from suspicion—but someone's a liar. Vandunk was seasick, is still confined to his cabin. Erh Tan is about today, for the first time. He was certainly sick. Your brother was in the engine-room at the time; the engineer was asleep in his own cabin and was wakened by the noise and confusion. The steward had just taken over the duties of cook and was aft in the galley. None of the men from for'ard were in or about the 'midships cabins. That's the layout; and somebody's a liar. No telling who it is, though. Not a shadow of suspicion."

"Where was Ali? Oh, yes; he was with us."

"Not all the time. But he has no weapon of any kind. Then, we don't know exactly when Andrews was murdered, so we can't definitely pin anyone down to the moment. The one sure thing is that everybody aboard is in a flutter."

"Vandunk had me come to his cabin," she said, hesitant. "This morning. He questioned me, very insistently, as though he suspected you might have done it."

Cairn laughed. "I more than half suspect he might have done it. Anyone might have! Did he look pretty green in the face?"

"He didn't look ill at all," she said. "He was well wrapped up, of course."

"Have you, personally, any suspicion of the faintest sort?"

"No," she answered in her cool way. "Not the least."

"Where'd you learn to speak Malay so well?"

"We've been out here a year, you know. And immediately we resolved to come out, we pitched in to learn it. Everyone does. It's an easy language."

CAIRN NODDED. One of the seamen, a Portuguese halfcaste named Souza, came up the ladder and saluted. Mynheer Vandunk would like to see the captain.

"I'm on duty until eight bells," said Cairn. "What were you doing around the cabins?"

"Me and Hilo Tom were put on brass polishing, sir. You done it."

"Right. Tell Mr. Vandunk I'll see him at eight bells." The man went back, and Cairn turned to Stella Tracey. "Wouldn't you feel better if you had a pistol about your cabin? You look to me like the sort of girl who could use a gun."

"Thanks, I am, and I have," she said, laughing. "Mr. Drift insisted that I should bring one along; he gave me one in Surabaya. A Webley. He said that it was by Mr. Vandunk's orders."

"Eh?" Cairn's gray eyes glittered suddenly. "Would you mind getting it and letting me have a look at it?"

"Gladly."

She went below, to return with a handbag in which the pistol lay. Cairn gave it a short examination, beyond sight of the helmsman. Brand new, never used, same calibre, fully loaded. He replaced it in the handbag, with a nod.

"Thank you. A good gun. Hello! So he's come to me, eh?"

Mynheer Vandunk, shawl about his neck, came nimbly up the ladder. He bowed and removed his hat momentarily to the girl, then gave Cairn a look.

"Can we step into the house for a moment and talk?" he said.

"If you like. No, don't go, Miss Tracey," Cairn replied. "We may need your cool head to solve some of our problems. I'm sure Mynheer Vandunk agrees."

Vandunk assented. As the girl had said, he did not look at all ill. Once shut away from the wind, with a mere shrug at the presence of the Malay quartermaster, Vandunk faced Cairn brusquely.

"I'm not satisfied about these murders, Cap'n. As you know, this crew was handpicked. None of our men could possibly have killed Lochaber and Andrews. That puts it squarely up to anyone outside our men. You yourself, your Malay servant, that plump Chinese supercargo—"

"And Miss Tracey and her brother," put in Cairn. "Dead right, Vandunk, from one viewpoint. We'll come back to that in a minute. First, since the cook was your man and tried to murder me, what have you to say about it?"

Vandunk's little shoe-button eyes glittered. "Do you dare accuse me?"

"Certainly. I accuse anyone. Mr. Drift shot the cook. Two of the men were on the spot. Both swore that the cook attacked Mr. Drift. Let that pass. It was Mr. Drift who found Andrews murdered. Maybe he murdered him and then came to give the alarm. I don't think so, mind; I say, it's possible. You might have done it. You've been laid up, but you look devilish healthy. You may as well face the possibilities all around."

Vandunk bit at a cheroot, then smiled slowly.

"1 see. You're nobody's fool, Cap'n. I stick to it that no one in our crowd committed those murders. I've done a bit of investigation. There's no such knife aboard—no kris *melala*. Either it was flung overboard, or it's hidden away. And I've checked something else. Lochaber and Andrews, as I told you, were at Coomassin. Possibly they were killed because of that fact—because of their treachery, as the natives there called it."

"More than likely; that would explain why Andrews was so startled, even afraid," said Cairn. "And that puts it up to one of your own men. Ali tells me he was never there in his life, told me so when I first engaged him. Some one of your own crowd up for'ard has put it over on you, Vandunk."

Vandunk was staggered. He scowled thoughtfully and then nodded.

"Possibly you've hit it. Frankly, I did think at first you were the killer."

"And I thought you might be; I still think so," said Cairn bluntly. "Not that I believe you were. I say, it's possible."

MISS TRACEY broke in upon the threatening silence with a bright laugh.

"I'll tell you what it all sounds like," she said cheerfully. "I've heard a good deal of talk at Singapore about the piracy up the coast. This sounds like one of the mysterious jobs pulled off by that man they call the Devil's Bosun! They say he has confederates aboard ships, you know, who murder the officers at the proper time."

Vandunk bit at his cheroot. His thick lips curved, merriment came back into his rather broad features—merriment, amusement that was a mask, but not humor.

"The Devil's Bosun!" he repeated, with a chuckle. "My dear Miss Tracey, that is all rot, really. Legend gets built up around some rascally pirate; he is given all sorts of attributes; every crime committed in the seven seas is laid at his door. As a matter of fact, no intelligent or even shrewd man would be a pirate, in this day of radio and sea-police. He couldn't get away with it."

"The Devil's Bosun does," said the girl. Vandunk shrugged.

"Nonsense; forgive me, but it is nonsense. Look at those pirates up around Bias Bay, within sight of Hongkong! Some genius was supposed to be at their head. When they were broken up, nothing of the sort was found. The same in this case. We have a number of piracies up the Celebes coast, and people jump to the conclusion that some person has contrived them all. No, no; it's quite unlikely. By the way, Cap'n, what do you know about this servant of yours? This Ali? Been with you long?"

"No," said Cairn. "He had a recommendation from Li Tock Lo in person; he used to be a Malay trader who had a ship of his own. He's a *raja*. That is, of good blood, a noble as opposed to a peasant. I think he's faithful. I know he has no weapon of any kind. That's really about all I know of him."

Vandunk nodded. "That's enough. Where is he from?"

"Kelantan, in the Malay States."

"I'm satisfied, then." Vandunk lit his cheroot. "We've checked up on every one of our men aboard; as you say, somebody's lying. Mr. Drift tells me that Erh Tan is a relative of Li Tock Lo. That rules him out. Looks like a plump young capon; not the sort to use a knife so well. We're blocked, that's all."

"There still remains the question of why your cook tried to poison me."

"I know. I can't explain that." Vandunk turned to Cairn, spreading out his hands. Earnestness suddenly sat in his face, his voice. "Cap'n, we're blocked; I can say no more. I'd give five thousand guilders, gold, if I could find the murderer of our two officers. I've spread that offer among the crew. Every man aboard is on the alert this moment."

Cairn stiffened. "Not your place to make the offer. You should have suggested it to me. I'm the captain aboard here, not you. You're here by sufferance."

"Eh?" exclaimed Vandunk. "I've chartered this ship, sir!"

"That has nothing to do with it. In future, remember the fact." Cairn smiled, and removed the offense of the words. The quartermaster turned to him and he nodded. Eight bells; four o'clock. "Now, mynheer, suppose we all have a regular English afternoon tea, eh? Mr. Drift will be up in a minute. Here he comes now. You'll join us, Miss Tracey? I'll have your brother as well—"

Vandunk assented. With the cheroot between his teeth, he could not very well claim illness.

Ali was sent for tea. Tracey joined them in the mess cabin, as soon as he had removed the marks of his labor; he grinned boyishly, was eager about his job. Vandunk threw off his wraps, and Stella Tracey soon had him talking. He revealed himself as a man of wide travel and information; but Cairn, who was watching him with attention, divined that he kept a continual restraint upon himself. Vandunk said frankly that he detested the sea, and once he reached Coomassin intended to stay there several years. He was, Cairn judged, a man of forty-five.

"Have you any plans in regard to the sultana there?" asked Stella Tracey. "I understand you have entire authority over the island."

VANDUNK ASSENTED. "Plans? No," he said slowly. "No. I shall act for the best interests of the island, of course. An unfortunate situation, with that woman of white blood. It may be that a native sultan would be better regarded by the people."

"But," put in Tracey, "I thought she was the heiress of the former sultan?"

Vandunk waved his cheroot and smiled. "Oh, yes; however,

I shall be guided by the resident there. It is impossible to predict conditions."

Cairn decided definitely that he did not like Mynheer Vandunk. The man was very shrewd, far more so than he appeared on the surface.

Later, when Ali was in his room, Cairn told the Malay about Lochaber and Andrews having been at Coomassin previously, and suggested that this might in some way lie behind their killing.

"That is true, tuan," said Ali reflectively. "I heard two of the men forward talking about it. It seems that those white men betrayed the sultan to the Dutch, although they had taken his salt and were in his service. It would not be strange if someone aboard here had killed them for that reason. Shall I try to find if any of the Malays forward come from those parts?"

"If you can find out, do so," Cairn said. "And I'd give a good deal to learn why the cook tried to poison me."

Ali took from his pouch a bit of leaf-wrapped betel paste, and mouthed it.

"Allah alone knows the truth, tuan! I have heard men talk about the time when Tuan Drift will be captain."

Cairn whistled. So the crew expected that Drift would be captain!

"And," went on Ali slowly, "at that time there will be many women aboard."

"Interesting," said Cairn drily. "Keep your ears open."

He went to the cabin of Erh Tan, knocked, and entered. The plump young yellow man was sitting up, still very pallid, but still very calm. Politeness over, Cairn spoke abruptly.

"Some of the crew seem to think that Mr. Drift will be captain before long. One attempt has been made to poison me. Two of the officers have been murdered. Now, if you have any suspicions, speculations, or guesses, I'd like to hear 'em."

Erh Tan smiled faintly.

"Captain Cairn, you think because I am Chinese, maybe I

guess something. You white men all think the Oriental people are very deep and shrewd. That is not so. We think differently, but we are far less shrewd than you. We are not deep and complex. Maybe we start a ball rolling, and that is all; we cannot tell where it will roll. Mynheer Vandunk hired this ship through his agent. Cash was paid, much cash. It is agreed that when cargo is handled, it is handled through the agents and associates of Li Tock Lo, in any port. I look after such interests. You look after the ship. It is very simple."

"It's too damned simple," Cairn said. "Suppose you and I were killed?"

"That would not matter. The ship is insured. She is old and has little value. No one would kill us in order to steal her. But how can I tell? A man walking in a fog has no advantage over a blind man."

No help here. The young fellow was a mass of sluggish inertia, at this moment anyhow. And yet he had suggested that Lochaber's wounds had been made by a certain kind of kris—an odd thing for a Straits Chinese living in Java to know.

"Who ever told you," asked Cairn, "what a kris *melala* was like?"

Erh Tan stared at him for a moment, then smiled again.

"You think it strange that I should know, eh? Well, that is natural. About a week ago I was dining with my relative Li Tock Lo. He had upon his desk a Malay kris. The handle was made from old yellow ivory, and the blade was inlaid with gold. Like that of any kris, the blade was wavy like a flame, but unlike most, it had a heavy ridge in the center, on either side of the blade. My honorable relative told me that this kind of kris was called *melala* and was only carried by chiefs, among the barbarians. I remembered it. When I saw the body of the engineer, the shape of the wounds showed they had been made by a similar weapon."

That was all; simple, naive, candid. No deep and crafty brain here. This brain, like its body, was plump and soft. Still, it had its points; it had remembered and spoken at the right moment. Erh Tan was no fool, but he was no very crafty Oriental, either.

CAIRN WENT away thoughtfully.

"Maybe we start a ball rolling, and that is all." The plump supercargo had expressed a profound truth there. But where, in this business, had anyone except Vandunk started a ball rolling? Nowhere, apparently.

There remained the little matter of the Webleys, and Cairn doggedly determined to go after this. When Mr. Drift relieved him at four the next morning, Cairn for a moment discussed the course, then beckoned Mr. Drift out to the lee of the bridge house. There was only a faint breeze, with the glass dropping fast and some heavy weather ahead before they sighted Celebes.

"I suppose you haven't a gun, Mr. Drift?" asked Cairn.

"Aye, sir, that I have," was the prompt response. Mr. Drift, with surprising rapidity, slipped an automatic from an armpit holster. Cairn took it, moved forward into the light for a moment, then returned to the other man, but kept the gun.

"The same, I see. How did you happen to give Lochaber two instead of one?"

"Two?" In the darkness, the brisk mate caught his breath. "Why, sir—"

"You wouldn't intimate that Lochaber lied to me about it?" Cairn said grimly.

"Oh, no, sir, not for a moment! You see, now, this was the way of it." Drift was evidently sparring for thought. "I got 'im one, but he didn't like the hang of it. Very particular, the old chief was, about such things. So I got him another that he liked better. That's how it was, Cap'n. You see, I'd 'ad a chance to pick up a couple fairish cheap in Surabaya."

"I see," Cairn said, and clicked off the safety catch of the gun in his hand. He shoved it suddenly against the other man. "Hands up, Drift! You'll lie your way to the gallows yet, if you don't watch out. You found Lochaber dead; you found Andrews dead. You've lied like hell about these Webleys—"

Mr. Drift was pressing back against the iron rail, his hands lifted.

"Good God, sir, you can't be saying I done it!" broke out his voice in a wail of acute horror. "Why, they was my friends, shipmates! I couldn't ha' done it, sir. Mr. Vandunk knows bloody well I couldn't."

"How does he know it?" snapped Cairn.

"Why, sir, it—it was me as got 'em to sign on!"

"Then Andrews lied when he said that Vandunk signed him and Lochaber on."

"I dunno, I dunno," cried Mr. Drift in desperate panic. "The three of us 'ad to get berths. I sent 'em to Vandunk, then 'e made me 'is agent, and that's the God's truth of it."

"You lie like hell," Cairn said grimly, and paused. "But I don't believe you're a murderer. I don't care a hang who signed you on. Let's have the truth about all these brand new Webley pistols you put aboard. Out with it, or I'll clap you into irons on a murder charge and you can talk to an Admiralty court."

In the darkness his voice was like the ring of steel. Then another voice broke in. Cairn started, and turned to see the figure of Vandunk approaching past the door of the pilot-house.

"What's all this, Cap'n? This talk about pistols—good heavens! Is that a pistol in your hand?"

"Mr. Drift has brought a number of Webley pistols aboard, and I want an explanation," said Cairn. "He's lied about it. Either he talks turkey, or I'll put him in irons for the murder of Andrews and Lochaber."

Vandunk halted. His voice rolled out silkily, calmly, with authority.

"That's absurd, Cap'n; they were friends for two or three years, all three of them. I looked them up. As for the pistols, I can explain that. I strictly ordered Mr. Drift to say nothing about it to a soul. I picked up a dozen new Webleys in Batavia and sent them to Mr. Drift, asking him to distribute them among our officers and to the Traceys as well. I thought we should have the officers armed. Later on, Mr. Drift wrote me that Li Tock Lo was sending arms aboard, so I knew my precautions were useless."

Cairn replaced the safety catch and handed the gun to the mate.

"You have the bridge, mister; go ahead," he observed. "And next time you lie to me, heaven help you! There'll be no excuse."

Mr. Drift ducked into the wheelhouse. Vandunk spoke with asperity.

"You appear jealous of your authority, Cap'n Cairn. I don't like it by half."

"I don't give a damn what you like," Cairn said quietly. "Aboard this ship, just one man gives orders, one man's responsible, one man is supreme. You should realize the fact, and not act as though you were also in command aboard here. Mr. Drift may have been your agent ashore. Here, he obeys me and no one else."

Vandunk sighed, laughed, and passed his arm in that of Cairn.

"You're right, Cap'n. I do forget that my authority doesn't extend here; the fault is mine. Come below and have a glass of Hollands with me."

"Thank you," Cairn replied, "but I don't drink until we're lying at Coomassin."

Mynheer Vandunk sighed again. "Cap'n, you're a man after my own heart, but a trifle apt to flare up. I'd like to speak honestly with you, as man to man. I'd like you to hear me out, keep yourself under control, remember that I'm speaking to you as a friend, and allow me to speak with the frankness of a friend. Yes or no?"

Cairn sensed a vibrance from the man, a subtle blend of power and character, a sober warning of something tremendously important in the wind. His dislike died out. He answered quietly.

"Very well. I'm not always so hasty as you seem to think."

"I know that, Cap'n. I like you because you don't apologize or excuse your words or actions. You're more or less unnerved by these murders. So am I. The death of Lochaber and Andrews gave me a frightful shock, more so than you can realize."

Vandunk was speaking the truth; his voice rang with it.

"Miss Tracey," he went on, "mentioned to me the photograph in your cabin of the Sultana Amina, as she is called. I may assume that you think the young woman very lovely, in which you are correct."

"The picture is, at all events," said Cairn cautiously.

"Yes. Men don't keep a picture around unless they're moved by it. Now, when I was so careful about a crew for this ship, don't you suppose I was equally careful about the master? I was, Mr. Cairn. I looked him up and down, I promise you."

Cairn felt a tingle of warning. He could guess what was coming.

"I know," resumed Vandunk, "that you've been with this line for three years; that you obtained your tickets very rapidly; that your Board of Trade license is correct—all under the name of Cairn. I may have heard other things, but I speak only of what I know."

"Meaning what?" asked Cairn.

"That I like you. What lies in your past, I don't care. Allow me, and I'll make your future my concern. I may tell you that this sultana must be removed and safely put out of the way of making trouble for the government. If you like her—take her. I can give her to you, and no one else can do so. Marry her, do what you like. Wealth goes with her. In return, you take my orders, cut loose from your present employers. You'll never regret it."

"What sort of orders?" Amazed, bewildered as he was, Cairn spoke quietly. Did this man know or guess his past—that he had been kicked out of the navy, was now under an assumed name? Very probably. "Dishonest orders, mynheer?"

VANDUNK LAUGHED softly. "Would you care what

sort of orders? Can you afford to care? I offer you the most beautiful woman in this part of the world, for a wife or what you like; and wealth. I offer you a future to replace that which you lost. No man can afford to question what sort of orders he gets. In the American navy, you question no orders. In the army, you accept orders. But I accept your challenge! Yes. You might consider yourself bound to do anything I might command. In government service, remember, there are unpleasant duties— such as getting rid of young and lovely women. If you refuse her, a far worse man must get her."

Cairn lit a cigarette. His brain was in a whirl. Shame and disgrace lay like a blanket upon his soul. So his past was known or guessed! And this Dutchman thought him reckless of honor—

Honor? To hell with honor. That lay far behind him. Cap'n Cairn was a good seaman, with a clean ticket, but with a damned poor future. Here was one ready-made for him. Were Vandunk the devil in person, it certainly would not matter; and he had spoken frankly. Then there was the girl to consider. All question of money aside, the right person could save her from a lot of things.

"Think it over, Cap'n," said Vandunk quietly. "There's no hurry."

"You've sprung it on me a bit unexpectedly," Cairn rejoined. "That's true. I'll not deny—well, let me be frank. I don't like your jumping at the conclusion that I'd have no scruples over doing the wrong sort of things. I would. Nothing lies in the past that I'm ashamed of; much that I regret bitterly."

"Think it over," Vandunk repeated. "I need you for, say, three months. Then you can cut loose and the future is yours, and a free one. Give me your answer when we sight Coomassin—but keep confidential what I said about the sultana. Agreed?"

"Agreed," said Cairn. "Good night."

CHAPTER IV

ALI CAME early to make up the bunk, while Cairn was shaving.

"Well, what's the news?"

"The news is good, tuan."

It was the mechanical Malay greeting, as empty of meaning as "Good morning." Ali expectorated his crimson betel-paste saliva carefully into the slop-basin and then grinned.

"Tuan, somebody would like to do you in."

The expression, in Malay, was identical with the English phrase.

"Who?" Cairn demanded.

"I could not find out. Last night when they thought me asleep, they talked of your death as of a thing expected. More, I could not find out. But one of those men, who was a true believer, spoke of having killed an infidel, a Christian."

Cairn swung around. One of the Malays, no doubt, for all these Malays were followers of Allah. Here was something definite at last.

"Who was the man? Did he say when? Which of the two officers did he kill?"

"Neither one, tuan." Ali went on speaking in Malay, evidently to make sure of what he was saying and to avoid mistakes. "He only spoke of it as a thing done, a thing which would insure his entry into paradise. It was good luck, he said, that on the very night we sailed, before the ship was yet far at sea, he had sent a Christian infidel to hell. That is something I do not understand, tuan, for neither of these two officers was killed that night."

Cairn stood as though paralyzed. His mind slipped back, and farther back, to the night they had sailed from Surabaya.

No, nothing had happened; no one had been missing then—no one.

"Ah!" The quick exclamation broke from him. Stella Tracey's story—the body that had fallen from the port—Mynheer Vandunk's explanation about his unfortunate servant who had taken too much bhang and opium! "But that man was—"

He checked himself, unwilling to say too much. Not a white man? How did he know? Probably Vandunk's servant had been a white man, a Dutchman. Probably the fellow had really been killed, and Vandunk had covered up the matter to save himself trouble. Which he had certainly done. The man had not been entered on the articles, and no trace of the killing, if it were such, now remained.

"A man fell overboard that night, Ali," said Cairn slowly. "But he was not one of the crew. I did not know he was a white man. Possibly he was."

No. Vandunk had very definitely said the man was a Malay. He had said the man was a victim of the disease called *lateh*, a nervous disorder which causes a man to commit violence and draw blood, spasmodically, almost without knowing it. Vandunk had made no mistake. Either Vandunk or this man up forward had lied. And it was not the man who had hoped to enter paradise by his deed; it was Vandunk.

"Well, no matter," said Cairn at length. "It is not my affair. It's got nothing to do with the murder of the two officers. And as for killing me, they have a long way to go before that happens."

"May Allah will it!" echoed Ali, and fell to work at the bunk.

CAIRN LOOKED at the picture on the shelf under the mirror, and went about his business in a dream that held his clear gray eyes unseeing. Even though the glass was down and weather whistling to clutch them in storm, he could think of nothing else. The face of that girl had bewitched him. The thought of her obsessed him.

The thought of her, torn from place and friends by an arrogant Dutch master, given over as a chattel to anyone who would take her, fired his blood with anger. Not *that* way would he have her from Vandunk's hand! He might not have her at all, in fact; he might not want her; she might not want him. It was all the most utter madness to think about. But there was the picture, there was her lovely face, to assure him it was no dream; and the offer from Vandunk.

His future free and clear, whether with a wife or not. His future; money in the bank, a chance to build and carve afresh with no more slaving for mere wages. At the cost of three months' forgetting. A cheap price! He'd be a fool to throw it over. Lord knows he'd been no stickler for honor! And the thought that he would be in government service was like opium, deadening the conscience.

The world owed him a bitter debt. For a thing he had never done, he had been chucked out of the navy, been given a chance to disappear and be marked down as dead. Another man, some other man, had done it, fastening the guilt on him; that other man—and Cairn had never known who he was—now walked a warship's deck in high career. Well, no use thinking about it. He'd never regain what he had lost, and did not want to regain it. That was all done with. Ahead lay a suddenly golden future. Vandunk would give the orders, he would carry them out.

"I'll do it; and to hell with regrets!" he told himself. "After all, only the fellow who comes out on top matters. You've got to step on somebody to get anywhere!"

Gray scud filled the sky, an ugly sea was coming up; the *Ta Ming*, high in ballast, rolled like sin and pitched like a devil. Cairn was getting a storm apron rigged at the break of the bridge when Stella Tracey joined him. She enjoyed the whip of spray and the lash of the wind, and the foaming seas beneath, now beginning to burst over the forward well deck.

"I want to ask you something," she said, as they stood in the lee of the pilot house. "Something personal. You remember the picture I saw in your cabin?"

"And that you mentioned to Vandunk?" said Cairn maliciously. "Yes."

Her cool blue eyes dwelt upon him for an instant.

"Was there any harm in my mentioning that lovely face?"

Cairn broke into a laugh. "Lord, no! It brought me good luck. Go on."

"I wondered if I might show it to my brother. You know, you weren't sure whether it was the sultana's picture. He knew her and would be able to identify her. I'm curious to know whether it's really her picture."

"So am I," said Cairn eagerly. "Yes; by all means! I can't leave the bridge until noon, however. If you like, here's the key of my cabin. The picture's on the shelf under the mirror."

She hesitated, then took the key with a nod.

"Thanks very much. By the way, when do we reach Coomassin?"

Cairn squinted at the sky. "Depends on this blow. With luck, tomorrow night or next morning. The old girl's pretty good on her pins, old as she is."

After all, he thought, he had only the word of two drunks as to that photograph. A lot might depend on it; if it were not a picture of Amina, he would need to know it. Good thing Miss Tracey had thought about it.

NOON WAS approaching, and the ship was wallowing stoutly along, when Stella Tracey came clawing up the ladder to the bridge again. She stood in the open lee doorway and made a peremptory gesture.

Even before she gestured, at first glimpse of her, Cairn's pulses leaped; he knew something was fearfully and dreadfully wrong. Every bit of color was gone from her face, and her blue eyes were ablaze. As they touched on him, they seemed to recoil, to shrink back from him in horror.

He hastened to obey her motion, to join her outside, alone.

"What's wrong?" he shouted at her ear. "You look as though you'd seen a ghost."

"Worse," she replied, and thrust the key into his hand. "Take that."

"What's up?" he demanded, puzzled by her manner. "Get the picture?"

She shook her head, her eyes staring at him.

"No. I fell over—a lurch of the ship. I fell on your bunk. You—"

The rest was swept away by a howl of wind. Cairn caught her arm, and she pulled free as though his touch burned her.

"Go look for yourself!" she cried at him, stridently. "Look under the edge of your bunk. Can't talk here."

Then she turned and slowly made her way down the ladder out of sight.

Cairn cursed in bewildered surmise. What the devil could she be talking about? Well, no matter now. Too much going on to pay any attention to the whimsies of a woman. Until eight bells, he must stick right here.

Before noon sounded, Mr. Drift was on the bridge, cool and brisk as ever, his bright eyes darting about. No noon sights today, of course. All going well below, and the glass steady; even rising a fraction. The blow would be over by next morning. They talked, compared notes on drift and windage, pricked over the chart. Eight bells sounded. The watches were changed.

"Blasted good meal waiting down there," said Mr. Drift cordially. "Eat hearty, sir! Good luck."

Cairn, on tenterhooks, hastened below at last. Before going to mess, he must see what it was all about. Miss Tracey's eyes still burned into him.

He unlocked his cabin, stepped inside, closed the door again. He could see nothing amiss. What had she said—to look under the edge of the bunk? Why, the woman must have been out of her head! Nothing wrong with the bunk. Nothing wrong with—with—

Good God!

A lurch of the deck threw Cairn sideways. He caught the edge of the bunk, sat down on the deck, and reached out to the thing that lay there just beneath the bunk. It was a knife, a short-handled, long-bladed knife, the blade wavy like a flame. A Malay kris, all stained and caked with dried blood.

The blade was not flat. It had a high, tapering ridge on either side. It was a kris *melala;* it was the knife that had killed Lochaber and Andrews. This was the dried blood of Andrews still upon it.

Cairn stared at the thing. What was it doing here in his cabin? It had not been here the previous night or he would have seen it. Or—or—

A sudden thought struck him. He lay flat on the deck, twisted his head beneath the bunk, looked up at it. Across the springs and the bottom of the mattress were dark smears. The knife had been hidden there, under the mattress, only to work out gradually. When Stella Tracey was flung off balance on the bunk, her weight must have knocked out the knife.

Cairn's brain struggled back to coherence. Hidden in his cabin—why? So that blame could be cast upon him?

For a moment the thought burned hotly within him, then died away. No, that was most unlikely. He had been here with Miss Tracey when Andrews was killed, and the knife had been stowed away here, red with blood. Perhaps before he came to his cabin and went to bed. Perhaps after. More likely before, though. It was improbable that the murderer could have hidden the knife under the mattress while he lay in bed with Stella Tracey sitting beside him.

While he lay here, Mr. Drift had come in, Erh Tan, Ali. No one else. No, the murderer must have been in the second mate's cabin when Andrews came off watch and walked in. Someone below here, not on deck. Finding this knife, knowing it must have been put here before the cabin was occupied, narrowed things down.

CAIRN LOOKED at the knife again. A short ivory handle, made to fit the small hand of a Malay. Beautiful old ivory, yellowed with age. A murderous ridged blade, such as only chiefs or great men would use, made of native Trengganu steel. Finely worked, this steel. Cairn rubbed it with his finger and saw yellow inlay. Gold. Arabic letters and arabesques inlaid in gold.

A sudden flame leaped through all his veins. He had the murderer at last!

Rising quickly, he went to the washstand and there cleansed the handle and part of the blade, washing off the dried blood, leaving the lower half of the kris as it had been. He thrust it under the blanket of his bunk, then made haste to the mess-cabin.

There he found Miss Tracey, her brother and Mynheer Vandunk, who was no longer affected by mal-de-mer. Cairn seated himself and met with a smile the coldly questioning blue eyes of the girl.

"Well, my friends," he said cheerfully, "thanks to Miss Tracey, here, I think I'm on the trail of the murderer of Lochaber and Andrews. I'll know in an hour or so. Miss Tracey, I'm going to ask you to accompany me, after lunch, to settle the matter."

She assented silently. An exclamation burst from Vandunk, just as Ali came into the cabin with his tray.

"What, Cap'n? You know who murdered 'em?"

Cairn nodded. "And I've got the weapon. Can't go into it now, until I make certain. So let it pass for the present." He glanced up and met the gaze of Ali fastened upon him, a wide and startled gaze. He smiled. "Ali! Remember the man whom you mentioned to me? The one who's headed for paradise? I want you to send him to my cabin at four bells—two o'clock. Nothing wrong; I merely want to ask him a few questions. How's Mr. Erh Tan today?"

"The Chinaman is improving, tuan," Ali said, with his usual

touch of contempt when mentioning the yellow race. "He has requested some food."

Cairn nodded and pitched into his meal.

"I say!" exclaimed young Tracey. "Couldn't you tip us off, Cap'n? We're all friends here, you know."

Cairn chuckled, met the shoe-button eyes of Vandunk, and winked.

"Are we? When Mynheer Vandunk had his doubts about me—and I had mine about him? Huh! Wait till it's definitely settled."

Under the impact of his decisive tone, the others laughed and yielded. Vandunk began to talk with Stella Tracey about rubber exports. Her brother, with his boyish manner, produced a clipping from his pocket, laughed, and thrust it at her.

"There you are, sis. You said you'd ask Mynheer Vandunk about it--"

He broke off, at his sister's angry flush. She caught at the clipping. Vandunk laughed and flung a question at her. Reluctantly, she gave him a glimpse of the clipping before tucking it out of sight.

"Nothing at all; silly curiosity," she said. "I saw this picture of you in an official gazette in Surabaya and kept the cutting. We decided it didn't look like you."

Vandunk's broad features contracted slightly. For an instant his eyes widened, and white showed around the pupils; then he broke into a hearty laugh.

"Oh! You're right about it," he said, chuckling. "It's an old picture, taken years ago when I was young and good-looking."

Cairn rose abruptly. "Ready, Miss Tracey? Let's go. Mynheer, I'll look you up in your cabin as soon as we know the rights of this."

Vandunk nodded silently. Cairn departed with Stella Tracey. She said nothing as she followed to Cairn's cabin. Her air was aloof but alert. Cairn unlocked his door and ushered her in, then took the kris from under the blanket. He wrapped it in a couple of towels and turned to her.

"By the way, would you mind letting me see that picture of Vandunk? I'm a bit curious about it."

She produced the clipping. "Keep it, if it interests you. I'm sorry my brother mentioned it before him. Just what do you propose doing about that kris?"

"You'll see." Cairn glanced at the clipping, which showed a face of pronounced aquiline features, then tucked it from sight. "Come along, please. My program will explain itself and avoid a lot of talk."

His Webley was already in his jacket pocket, hanging heavily.

H E   L E D   the way to the cabin of Erh Tan and knocked. At the response, he opened the door. The plump young Chinese, now not so plump, was sitting up in his berth.

"Miss Tracey is here," said Cairn, "We may come in? Thanks. I'd like a word with you, and it's rather important."

Erh Tan protested the disarray of his room, but Cairn ignored him. When the door was closed, he spoke calmly, affably.

"Do you remember telling me of having seen a certain kris lying on the desk of your relative, Li Tock Lo, in Surabaya?"

Erh Tan remembered. He told of it again, exactly as he had told Cairn on the previous occasion, and described the kris. There was wonder in his face as he spoke, and a certain perplexity.

"That," said Cairn, "was about a week before we sailed, you said. Did you ever see the kris again?"

"Yes," said Erh Tan. "A day or two later, I noticed it, in the same place. I may have seen it on other occasions, but do not recall it."

A heightened color had risen in the cheeks of Stella Tracey.

"You haven't left your cabin for several days, I think?" asked Cairn.

"I have been ill." Erh Tan gestured helplessly. "That day when

Ali told me you were poisoned, I went over to your cabin. It was the only time I have been out of the room."

Cairn laid bare the kris. "Is this the same weapon?"

Erh Tan looked at it and caught his breath. The pallor of his rotund face deepened. His eyes sharpened and drove suddenly at Cairn.

"That's it, Captain!" he exclaimed. "The same, the same! But how—"

"Exactly. How?" repeated Cairn grimly. "This was found hidden in my cabin, with the blood of Andrews still on it. And I don't think it walked aboard of itself. You've been below here. You're the only person, apparently, who might have murdered Mr. Andrews, hidden the knife in my room, and then returned here before I took to my bed that day. As to the murder of Lochaber—"

For a long moment Erh Tan stared up at him, with agitation working in the plump features. Then those features settled into lines of calm. The oblique eyes quieted. Cairn was perfectly acquainted with this phenomenon, so familiar to any who have had intimate dealings with the Chinese. Erh Tan had simply "retired within himself," as his people express it. He had cast a politely blank veil over his intercourse with the whites before him.

"I cannot explain," he said with a strange dignity. "I understand what you think. I cannot argue against it. I have been very ill here, and certainly would not have desired to kill anyone. I know nothing more about the kris than what I have already told you."

"Don't be a fool," said Cairn roughly. "The facts are against you—"

"I think Erh Tan has told us the truth, Captain," intervened Stella Tracey of a sudden. Cairn flung her an irritated glance.

"What? It's impossible that anyone else should have brought this kris aboard."

"You don't know that it is," she returned, and smiled. "You

think it impossible; that does not make it so. Erh Tan would never have mentioned the kris to you, had he been guilty."

Cairn nodded. "Perhaps; perhaps not. You prefer to think me the guilty one?"

"Don't be silly." Her blue eyes warmed upon him. "I think nothing of the sort. Li Tock Lo is the person to ask about this weapon."

"Right. None the less," said Cairn, "I must put you under arrest and confine you to this cabin, Erh Tan. Agree, and I'll not charge you openly with the murders, until we can communicate with Li. Is there a cable station at Coomassin?"

"There is nothing," said the young Chinese calmly. "Macassar would be the nearest point from which you could reach Surabaya. Your proposal is equitable. I accept."

CAIRN NODDED, ushered Miss Tracey out, locked the door and pocketed the key. The ship was lurching badly. He caught the hand-rail in the passage and looked at the English girl.

"Blessed if I know what to think!" he said slowly. "I'm tempted to believe him, and yet the facts—"

"You mean, the facts that we can see," she cut in. "You've brought me into this; let's be quite frank. You're not the type of man to commit murders, or in such a manner. That's why I was so horrified at finding the knife. Now, Erh Tan isn't the right type, either. He's really been very ill. Let the matter rest for the present as it is. Let me go and see Vandunk and tell him just what's happened; I think I can make him see the thing aright."

Cairn was silent for a moment. Oddly enough, into his mind flitted the words of Erh Tan: "Maybe we start a ball rolling, and that is all; we cannot tell where it will roll." Had somebody started some ball rolling here? What did Li Tock Lo know about this peculiar kris?

"Very well," Cairn said slowly. "Remember, the day Lochaber was killed, Erh Tan was up and about for the first time. Then he became seasick again, as he is now. It doesn't look so good for him. However, have it your own way."

"Thank you." She put out her hand, frankly. Cairn gave her a firm grip, met her cool blue eyes, and then she was gone.

Cairn went to his own cabin, put the kris out of sight, and started for a turn on the bridge. As he emerged from the passage and went to the foot of the ladder, he caught a sudden terrific commotion on the forward well deck below. He swung around, startled.

A knot of the men there, careless of the flying spray and water, were tangling in mad and insensate battle. Yells rang on the wind, knives were flashing; half a dozen men were hotly swarming in the knot. Then a flying figure came down past Cairn, caught the lower ladder, hit the deck, and went into the mass of them. It was Mr. Drift.

Cairn was stupefied at the swiftness, the savagery, of the mate's action. Mr. Drift went into them barehanded. The knot disintegrated into groaning men. One of them rushed in with ready knife. A shot spanged out and the man fell. Pistol in hand, Mr. Drift kicked the others about their business and then re-turned, leaving the dead man to be tended by the others. At the top of the ladder, Cairn met him.

"Mister, that was a revelation! Did you kill that chap?"

"Aye, sir." Mr. Drift laughed shortly. "A bad actor, that Merah; he'd run amok and knifed two of the other men. When those brown monkeys run amok, they're done. They're bound for paradise, and the quicker the better. He was a proper bad 'un. Shall I log it?"

"Of course. All right above?"

"Quite, sir. Weather breaking a bit and the glass rising."

Cairn went back to his cabin. He had forgotten his instruc-tions to Ali, and meant to snatch an hour's sleep. First, he took out the clipping, the picture of Vandunk, and put it on his table. He stared down at it, frowning.

Younger? No. Not like Vandunk at all. A high-nosed, aqui-

line face with large eyes; a different man altogether. He thought
of Vandunk's expression at catching sight of the picture. Queer!
Yet the man had laughed it off quite naturally.

Four bells sounded; two o'clock. A knock, and Ali came into
the cabin. Cairn looked up.

"Hello! I forgot about that order—where's the man?"

"Dead, tuan." Ali came forward and squatted down, crushed
a wad of betel-paste and slipped it into his mouth. "It was the
man Merah, a Malay from Kedah, who ran amok a little while
ago and was shot by Tuan Drift."

"Eh? You mean that he was the same who boasted of having
killed a Christian?"

"The same, tuan." Ali chewed in silence for a space, his bright
old eyes fastened on Cairn. Then: "Tuan kapitan! When I was
a young man, I was a ship captain and owner of ships. Then I
went to England for a time. I know much about ships. Tuan
Vandunk has charts in his room and has been working over
them. On one is Coomassin."

"That's natural," Cairn said absently. "He's taking command
there for the Dutch government. I thought you knew this. It's
no secret."

"When you were on the bridge this morning, tuan, two men
were in the cabin of Tuan Vandunk for a long time, talking with
him. One was Tuan Drift. The other was Sabok, the quartermaster."

Cairn jerked awake. "Eh? In Vandunk's cabin—you're sure?"

ALI GRINNED unpleasantly. "If I do the work of a
mongrel dog, at least I have a dog's scent—and teeth."

Well, why not? Drift had been the man's agent. No harm in
one of the quartermasters coming along for a talk—no harm,
but damned queer just the same. It was off balance entirely.
Cairn began to stride up and down the cabin, knees giving to
the thrust of the deck, a frown ridging his forehead, thinning
his gray eyes.

"Any more word for'ard about my approaching death?" he shot out.

"None, tuan."

Cairn felt irritated with the man. He had the sense of being up against a blank wall here, as though this Malay knew a lot that remained unuttered.

"When you take any food to Mr. Erh Tan, get the key from me," he said. "He's locked into his cabin for the present. That's all. You may go."

Ali stood up. His gaze struck upon the table, upon the clipping lying there, upon the pictured face. A sharp glitter came into his eyes, as though of recognition. As he started to speak, came a rap at the door and the voice of Tracey.

"You here, Captain Cairn? May I come in?"

"Come in," sang out Cairn, and Tracey entered, laughing, blond, boyish. Ali took his departure.

"Cigarette?" Tracey proffered his case, struck a match, and sat on the edge of the bunk. "Well, how d'you like your amateur engineer?"

Cairn smiled. "He's open to congratulations. All well down below?"

"Smooth as smooth. Good old engines she's got." Tracey leaned forward earnestly. "Look here, sir; one of the stories about the Devil's Bosun goes that he's a chap named Patterson who was kicked out of the Shanghai Merchants' line a couple of years back. Never been proven, y'know. But a bally odd thing happened when I came off duty at eight bells. I turned back, having forgotten my cigarette case, and that halfbreed engineer was speaking to the bridge. He didn't know I was coming down the gratings, never saw me in fact. I heard him say, 'Tell Cap'n Patterson about it.' That was all. It's utter rot, of course, but—well, I thought I'd mention it."

Cairn's brows lifted. Mr. Drift had taken over the bridge at that time.

"Patterson? An unlikely name to mistake, I admit," he said

slowly. "You think we have the Devil's Bosun aboard? Why'd he be aboard us?"

Tracey leaned back and shook his head.

"I can't see, of course. Still, I was rather certain I'd caught the name aright. With these murders and all, you know—Well, I'll be off. Hope you don't think me too much of an ass to fetch such a story—"

"On the contrary," said Cairn, "I'm glad you did. I don't know what to make of it, for a fact. We've no pirates aboard. Not a chance; Mynheer Vandunk picked each man carefully. Even looked me up," and he grimaced wrily. "No, I don't think we need worry about the Devil's Bosun this trip, Tracey. But keep your ears open, by all means. So far we've drawn pretty blank, but no telling what may turn up."

Tracey departed. Almost instantly, Ali knocked and re-entered, as though he had been waiting outside the door. He slid forward and touched the clipping that still lay on the table.

"Tuan!" he exclaimed in his harsh Malay. "This man came aboard the night we sailed. I have not seen him since then. I saw him carried aboard. I was watching Tuan Vandunk come. This man was carried into his cabin after him; his hat fell off and I saw his face. Where is he now?".

Cairn swung around. For a moment he was incapable of speech, as the import of the words drifted across his mind. Vandunk's servant was a white man after all, then—no, impossible!

"Ali! You don't know what you're saying," he exclaimed quickly. "Not this man. Not this man of the picture!"

"It is the face of the white man who was carried into Tuan Vandunk's cabin," the Malay exclaimed vehemently. "I call Allah to witness that I speak truth, tuan kapitan! I saw his face before the door slammed. He has not been about the ship since then. He is the man whom Merah killed, the Christian—"

CAIRN FELT stifled. "All right. Clear out of here and let me think," he ordered. Ali drew back, blinking at him; a rush of blood had suffused Cairn's face, his eyes were wild, his manner was strange. He struggled to keep himself under control, to meet this thing sanely. He heard the door close, knew he was alone. He came forward and looked down at the picture on the table.

Incredible? It was insane. And yet there was no mistaking it.

Here was a picture of the man who had been carried limply aboard, and who had later been killed and dropped out of Vandunk's port. This frightful and unbelievable fact was the key to everything. Cairn's brain raced back, picked up details as he stood there.

The real Mynheer Vandunk had been bound for Coomassin, no mistake about that. Mr. Drift might have been his agent; probably was not. With an appalling effrontery, all the details had been arranged and dovetailed. Just how, did not matter now; it had been managed superbly. That little matter of the train from Batavia having been missed, gave the clue. Mynheer Vandunk had left Batavia—but he had not reached Surabaya consciously. Another man had taken his place.

Another man had come aboard ship in the early morning hours, taking his name; another man, muffled to the eyes. The real Vandunk had been lugged aboard, and later knifed and thrown into the ocean. Coldblooded, efficient cruelty! Dead men tell no tales.

Handpicked crew? A bitter, wild laugh burst from Cairn.

"Who's this fellow, then?" he muttered. "Who's this man posing as Vandunk—this infernally clever rat who's been running the whole show, who has Vandunk's papers, who's taken his place? By the lord Harry, who else could it be? Tracey put a name to him—Patterson."

The whole thing lay clear to him now. This man who called himself Mynheer Vandunk was in reality this Devil's Bosun.

CHAPTER V

NO SLEEP now for Cairn.

Oblivious of time, he dropped into a chair, put his head in his hands, and thought everything out with dreadful clarity. How plain now did each detail stand out! That Mr. Drift should have killed his two fellow-officers was impossible. Those two murders had nearly knocked everything haywire for the Devil's Bosun.

Drift had shot the cook, yes—shot him before he could talk, give anything away. He had been ordered to poison Cairn. The captain was the only person aboard who stood between Drift and complete command of the ship.

All such little details were explained now with horrible precision. They no longer mattered. Nothing in the past mattered. Those two murders were still unexplained, but they could wait. A pity the killer had not murdered the false Vandunk also, and Mr. Drift to boot!

Nothing mattered now except the future. This mattered terribly.

Imagination awake, Cairn could visualize what sort of a job this was on which the Devil's Bosun was embarked. A tremendous thing, an incredibly brazen thing, yet one that had every chance of success.

As Mynheer Vandunk, to steam up to Coomassin, invite the resident aboard and lock him up, then calmly loot the whole blessed place, from sultan's palace to the godowns. And do it under the power of Dutch authority, with the soldiers of the garrison to help. Then steam away and—what? Well, the Devil's Bosun would not have a hard job to lose himself, ship and crew, behind some far horizon.

A staggering conception, this, fit for a Drake, a Morgan, or any other looter of buccaneering days. All kinds of angles and

possibilities to it, if handled by a ruthless and efficient master. And who was to stop it, even now?

Cairn's nails dug into his palms as he sat there forcing down wild impulse, controlling himself, trying desperately to grapple with the situation as it was revealed to him. He needed his head, all of it; coolness, resource, daring. Just now he was lone-handed. A word, a look, and he was lost. He must guard himself with a tremendous caution, must meet craft with craft.

Sweat burst out on his forehead. Stella Tracey and her brother—what of them? They had corresponded with the real Vandunk, but had not met him. The Devil's Bosun had been forced to include them in his plans. Two pawns he could scrap anytime. Yes, everything had been carried off with a diabolic cleverness. Even Li Tock Lo had been taken in—that man had sensed something amiss, but had been taken in just the same.

"Good God!" groaned Cairn. "What am I up against—what can I hope to do? This devil has shipped his whole gang of cut-throats—"

HE STARTED abruptly, remembering his own case. More infernal shrewdness there. Patterson, to give the Devil's Bosun his true name, had at first marked Cairn for death. Then, two of his officers gone, he had decided to incorporate Cairn in his plan and use him. A man kicked out of the navy, living under a false name, dreaming of a beautiful face—why not? And Cairn groaned again, thinking how nearly right this reasoning had been.

No cable at Coomassin, no radio aboard ship, nothing. A clean sweep.

Cairn started up, hand going to Webley, hot flame in his brain. Walk into that cabin and pistol the devil—no, no! For God's sake keep cool! He dropped into his chair again, bony hands clenched, face tortured, eyes haggard and bloodshot. Mr. Drift had no doubt smuggled arms aboard for the whole crowd.

Wiping the sweat from his face, Cairn tried frantically to get his brain at work again, and managed to do it. He had to reckon up chances. He had to make some plan. Did Erh Tan suspect something? Was that why he had murdered Lochaber and Andrews? No matter. That young Chinaman was of no help here.

Tracey and his sister—they could be relied on to the utmost. But Tracey was too young. He'd give the thing away; no telling him. Stella, yes; she was worth a dozen of the brother. She had to know. And Ali would be true steel. So pitifully few and useless!

Cairn thought of the Irish whiskey in the locker, started up, sank down again. No; not now. Not a drop. Here was crisis. Keep a clear head!

What help at Coomassin? Probably little. A Dutch resident and a handful of native sepoys. A girl sultana—the thought of her face plucked at him, set his pulses twitching. For the love of God, think it out, plan something! Don't sit here like a bump on a log—do something! You're the only one who knows, you fool!

A knock at the door, repeated. Cairn called out hoarsely. The door opened to show Sabok, the halfbreed Malay quartermaster.

"Eight bells is past, tuan kapitan. Tuan Drift says—ya Allah! Is the tuan ill?"

"Yes." Cairn caught sight of himself in the mirror, disheveled, hair every way, face drawn and strained and gray. "Tell Tuan Drift I'll be up presently—ask him to keep the deck till I come. Half an hour."

Sabok departed, lithe and competent—and deadly. Deadly, every man of them! Pirates and murderers, the whole gang of the Devil's Bosun!

CAIRN STRAIGHTENED up a bit, slapped the Webley in his pocket, and walked out. He went to the cabin of

Erh Tan, unlocked the door, and stepped in. From his bunk, the plump young Chinaman regarded him blandly, placidly.

"I know now why you killed those two devils," Cairn said jerkily, abruptly. "I wish to hell you'd gone farther, and killed the Devil's Bosun himself! You needn't gawk at me. I know all about it. I've just learned the truth. Stay here, lay low, and I'll talk with you later. No chance now."

Erh Tan looked stupefied. "But I did not kill them!" lifted his plaintive voice. Cairn made an impatient gesture and stepped out of the cabin, locking the door again. The damned young fool was no good anyhow—queer that he should have been able to knife two of the worst cut-throats afloat! Still, one never can tell about these softies. The fellows who look the meekest may be the worst fighters. Li Tock Lo had said the same thing, somehow, "The strongest forces in the world are often those which appear the weakest." Wise old chap, Li.

What now? Hold everything; never mind the smash inside! Get to work, don't let a soul suspect. Meet these devils on their own ground, with their own weapons. The resolution was sharp and swift. Here was duty to be done, a ship to be saved, a woman to be saved, God only knew what to be saved at Coomassin. Move, blast you!

Cairn came up to the bridge. Mr. Drift, with his drooping mustaches and red nose and bright eyes, peered at him and nodded:

"Ill, sir? Not seasick, surely?"

"Still feeling a bit queer from that strychnia," said Cairn. "All right now."

Presently Mr. Drift was gone. Cairn stood out in the wind and spray; it blew him clean and whole and sane again. From the break of the bridge he looked down on the forward well deck. His eyes narrowed at sight of the men there, as the *Ta Ming* lifted and swooped and plunged afresh. Deadly, every man of them; armed, every man of them. One false move, and he was done for. And not himself alone.

Cairn was still standing there, feet wide apart, when Stella Tracey came up the starboard ladder. Her yellow hair was blowing and color was in her face from the wind and spray. The seas were going down, the wind was lessening, and sun was struggling through the western sky.

Meeting the gaze of Cairn, she came to a dead halt on the topmost step and looked steadily at him.

"What happened?" she demanded. "You look ten years older than when I last saw you. You haven't turned to stone by some accident?"

Cairn was about to answer when he caught a squeal from the speaking-tube. He turned and strode into the pilot-house. Another squeal. He replied with a crisp question. An excited Malay voice made response. The quartermaster at the wheel, who caught the words, rolled his eyes at Stella Tracey, in the open doorway.

Cairn felt suddenly sick. "Have him carried up to his cabin," he said, and turned to the woman watching him. He forced the words, hoarsely. "Your brother; fell from the gratings. You'd better go down. I'll be right along."

She turned and fled, wordless, stricken.

Cairn lit a cigarette; his fingers did not shake. He was suddenly sure of himself now. Things were at zero. He was glad that he had not told her before this blow fell, for she might have given the secret away. Turned to stone, eh? Yes; he must play the game like a stone man, indeed. No emotion. Pitiless, ruthless as the Devil's Bosun himself. Get rid of Mr. Drift first of all.

"By God, let 'em have what they've asked for!" grunted Cairn, and went below.

S O M E O F the black gang were bringing a covered thing into Tracey's cabin. He went directly to that of the halfcaste engineer, knocked, entered, woke the man from sleep, spoke harshly.

"Mr. Tracey's been hurt. Get below and take charge. Double

watches for you, but it's only till tomorrow. We'll sight the Celebes coast before dark. Stay on the job, and if anything goes wrong I'll kill you."

He went to the cabins in the other passage. The stokers were departing. He found Stella Tracey standing by her brother's bunk; the form there was covered over, and Cairn knew the worst. Tracey was dead.

"Accident?" he asked.

She nodded, staring at him, white-lipped but dry of eye. Cairn removed his cap and departed, closing the door. Outside, he came on Vandunk—so he must still think of the man. They came face to face.

Suddenly Vandunk took a step back. Cairn smiled grimly.

"Tracey fell from a grating—killed," he said. "I have the deck. Will you come up when you get a chance?"

"In ten minutes," said the other. "Anything I can do—for her?"

"Best leave her alone." With this, Cairn went back to the bridge. He liked to think of how Vandunk had abruptly stepped back from his eyes, as though fearing a blow. Still, that was bad business. It might warn the fellow.

When Vandunk came up the ladder, a thin shrill cry was echoing out from forward. Cairn clapped the Devil's Bosun on the shoulder and pointed. The sunset light fell upon blue dots on the eastern horizon.

"Peaks of Celebes," he exclaimed warmly. "Do your heart good, mynheer?"

Vandunk laughed, nodded, took his arm and walked him into the pilot house. Cairn turned to the quartermaster and spoke in Malay.

"I'll watch your course. Go down, find the steward Ali, and tell him I want some coffee up here in twenty minutes, and a bite to eat."

The man slipped away. Cairn lit another cigarette.

"No use waiting, mynheer," he said quietly. "I've thought things over. I'd be a fool to turn you down."

"You would," assented the other, his little blade eyes probing Cairn. "Mind one thing, though. No protests; I don't care for arguments."

Cairn nodded. "I get you. There'll be no protests; why should I give a damn, once I make up my mind? It's a bargain. Agreed?"

"Agreed," echoed the other, beaming. "By the way, you're two points off your course, I think."

Cairn corrected the course, laughed shortly. "Spoken like a seaman."

"I've had some experience, Captain. How did this accident happen to Tracey?"

"I've no idea."

Vandunk stepped to the engine-room tube, called down, listened.

"Slipped on the grating and fell. Poor fellow! Too bad, financially; he was a director in the Malayan Rubber Industries concern. We must have the burial without delay, I presume. Shall I arrange with his sister?"

"If you'll be so good," Cairn said. "Sunrise, perhaps."

Vandunk assented. "Won't you step down and have a drink with me?"

"No drinking till Coomassin. Then I'll go on a bender."

The other laughed and was gone, as the quartermaster reappeared.

Twenty minutes later, Ali brought up sandwiches and coffee. Cairn accompanied him outside, exchanged a word with him at the ladder, and returned. An accident, yes; nothing underhand about this death, it appeared. Too bad, financially, had said Vandunk; the man must have had some idea of turning Tracey's financial position to his own gain.

VANDUNK SHOWED up at mess, alone with Cairn, for a purpose.

"Miss Tracey told me today about Erh Tan," he said abruptly, when Ali was out of the way. "Hanged if I know what to say. D'you think he turned the trick?"

"Yes," said Cairn. "Nothing else to think."

"Exactly." The man's face changed, the subtly cruel eyes widened. "Then let it wait. Do nothing. Take things slow."

Cairn nodded. He caught a flash from the eyes, from the brain before him. He saw this man in a new light now; the swift changes of that face could be comprehended. He could guess what the Devil's Bosun would do with the man who had knifed two of his officers. And, to himself, he smiled.

Later, in his own cabin, Ali appeared and shut the door. Cairn beckoned him, and uncovered the kris with the long ridged blade. Ali blinked.

"This knife killed the two officers," said Cairn. "The man who did it is Erh Tan. And now let us talk together, servant of the Prophet! You are faithful to your salt; yet it is not as a servant that I would greet you, but as a raja, a man among men, a friend, Tuan Ali."

"That is good, tuan," said the Malay, as one equal to another.

"Mynheer Vandunk is a pirate, and this crew are all his men," Cairn said very bluntly. "The real Tuan Vandunk was killed and thrown overboard the night we left Surabaya. Now it is known that Erh Tan killed those two officers, therefore I think something will happen to him tonight. You and I must await the hunters, and the burden of watching is yours. When any man goes to the cabin of Erh Tan, call me."

Ali grinned happily.

"Very well, tuan. Who is on our side besides this young fat yellow pig?"

"No one, except Miss Tracey." Cairn lit a cigarette. "These men go to Coomassin to loot it. I have been promised the sultana and much wealth as my share, for I have thrown dust in their eyes."

"Then it was not a crime to kill those two officers?"

"It's about the best thing that young Chinese ever did."

"He did not do it, tuan."

"What?" Cairn stiffened. "Do you know who did it?"

Ali smiled grimly. His old eyes were alight, and his fingers crept about the ivory handle of the kris with a loving, fondling caress.

"It was I who killed them, tuan, and hid the kris under your mattress where none would seek it."

Cairn caught his breath. Ali was the murderer! And it had never occurred to him!

"Is this some lie?"

"By Allah, do I lie to a friend?" said the old Malay proudly. "As to why I killed them, that is my affair; let us not speak of it."

"But it's impossible! Man, that kris belonged to Li Tock Lo. Young Erh brought it aboard here."

"Not he, tuan, but I. Li Tock Lo gave it to me when he told me about you and sent me to become your servant."

CAIRN WHISTLED slowly. "Sent you, did he? Then it was no accident that you applied to me?"

"None," Ali rejoined, impassive. "The Dutch officials—may they rot in hell!—put me in prison. I escaped. Li Tock Lo helped me to get away, and took this means of doing it. The kris was one that had belonged to me in other days. He gave it back to me as a parting gift. There, tuan, is the story."

The story? Not a third of it, not a tenth of it, as Cairn very well knew; but the story as Ali desired him to know it.

Cairn lit another cigarette, frowning at the smoke-trail. All in a moment, his whole scheme of things was forced to a right-about. This old Malay was undoubtedly some criminal, though perhaps not guilty of actual crime, and shrewd old Li had helped him escape. Why had he knifed two men aboard here? No telling. They must have recognized him—that was a shrewd dodge, about the facial bandage. Well, all this did not matter.

Erh Tan, then, was just what he seemed, and no more. But now above all Vandunk would certainly want the plump young Chinese put out of the way. The Devil's Bosun was not going to have Erh Tan arrested and charged with murder—not much!

Cairn remembered what Erh Tan had said, "Maybe we start a ball rolling—" And fat old Li Tock Lo had done just that, started a ball rolling when he got Cairn to take this Malay out of danger. Yes—Andrews had recognized Ali, or had nearly recognized him. Cairn remembered now. That was why Andrews had been killed.

"All right; I've got to get some sleep," said Cairn abruptly, and pinched out his cigarette. "Erh Tan's cabin is locked. Probably someone will come to kill him, with or without a key. Any skeleton keys can unlock these ancient doors. Watch. When anyone comes, call me. Can you manage it?"

Ali smiled grimly. "One who hunts the tiger in a canebrake, can keep watch on men aboard ship, tuan. Leave your door open. Shall I keep the kris?"

"Keep it," said Cairn.

Ali departed.

Cairn dropped on his bunk; he was asleep instantly, worn out in mind and body. That Ali was to be fully trusted, he was convinced. Criminal or not, about the man was a simple dignity that told its own story. And, where killing was concerned, any Malay was like a dog on the scent of fox.

IN THE darkness, Cairn wakened to a touch on his face. He stirred, his senses woke; he heard a voice in Malay at his ear, speaking softly.

"Tuan, the hunter comes. I turned off most of the deck lights. No time to waste."

Like a shadow, Ali was gone.

Cairn was after him in stocking feet, out into the dim-lit passage. It must be close to midnight, eight bells. Around the turn, where Ali waited; there, at the door of Erh Tan's cabin, appeared a vague dark shape working at the lock. Who it was, Cairn could not tell. He did not delay to find out.

The cabin door swung open. The man there suddenly became aware of Cairn's silent approach and whirled around. A long knife gleamed—too late! Cairn had him.

Had him by the knife wrist, wrenched him around, got arm under throat—held him thus despite struggles. It was Sabok the quartermaster. Like a snake, he thrashed and struggled, like a snake held in a relentless and inexorable grip. His knife-arm was bent back, his throat and head were stretched back, and farther back. All his pliant effort was of no avail.

A hoarse, thick cry issued from his throat, muffled and incoherent beneath that strangling arm. His left hand tore frantically and vainly at his captor. Foam flecked his lips and his eyes bulged. His feet thrashed sharply, desperately. Cairn held him in a fearful purchase to which all his own struggles lent new weight; either arm or neck must go.

Suddenly, wildly, Sabok made a frightful contortion that shook his whole body, lifted it from the floor. It dropped again. There was a queer dull sound. His corded sinew relaxed and became limp. Cairn realized the truth, and let him go—the force of that terrific muscular spasm had done its own work. The man's neck was broken.

"Ya Allah!" exclaimed Ali, staring down at the dead thing. "Tuan, you slew him without a weapon—"

"Help me get him overboard," said Cairn, breathing hard. "Into the cabin of Tuan Andrews, and out through the port there."

He shut and locked again the door of Erh Tan, who had apparently not wakened, then with Ali's assistance removed Sabok from the scene of his mortal endeavors. Presently it was done. Eight bells, midnight, sounded. Cairn, still panting from that deathly embrace, sought the bridge.

He spoke pleasantly with Mr. Drift, thinking all the while how Mr. Drift had so efficiently removed both the cook and the poor devil who had run amok—the man Merah, who had gained paradise at the expense of the real Vandunk, and who might have been tempted to talk further about it if left alive.

He joined in Mr. Drift's irritated wonder that Sabok did not come to relieve the other quartermaster. Although he did not say so, he could quite sympathize with Mr. Drift, for it was evident that Sabok had been one of the best men belonging to the Devil's Bosun. At length another man from the watch was called to the bridge, and the chief officer departed briskly to institute an inquiry.

CAIRN FACED the early morning hours more equably. Almost blithely, indeed, with a return of his old jaunty poise and readiness for anything. The encounter with Sabok had been like a safety-valve. He was able to look at the situation with a clearer eye. He had fully intended to strike his first blow at Mr. Drift, but this no longer seemed essential to him. After all, he was scarcely in a position to make open war, and he might much better hope to accomplish something by using his head, rather than his hands.

He thought the thing out as the *Ta Ming* bored through the darkness toward the Celebes coast and Coomassin. Blow upon blow had fallen, but there was no crisis. He was accepted as an ally of the Devil's Bosun, and this meant that he could yet hold the game in his own grip. There were other factors to consider—the sultana ahead, the Dutch resident. Ah—the resident! Suddenly Cairn realized that there might lie the key to everything, and why. The thought was bracing.

Sunrise glittered, the *Ta Ming* hove to in a glory of golden radiance, and the body of Tracey was committed to the deep. Cairn read the burial service, with Vandunk standing bareheaded. Stella Tracey looking on with hot, dry eyes, the crew at attention. Then it was over, and the old ship plunging forward again, and Coomassin close at hand.

If there were any agitation, any uneasiness, over the disappearance of Sabok, Cairn could not discern it. The man had vanished; that was all. Presumably a suicide. Erh Tan remained confined to his cabin. But Cairn, who had been studying the detailed chart of the Coomassin anchorage through the night, spoke quickly with Ali when he came off watch, before the funeral; and spoke with him again before breakfast.

"Can you do it?" demanded Cairn.

"Yes, tuan," and the eyes of the Malay glittered at him. "I understand clearly, and it shall be done as you desire. Indeed, it is the only thing to do."

"And be sure to reach the resident in person," Cairn cautioned him. "He must know at the outset just who this Vandunk really is."

"I understand, tuan," said Ali, with a deep chuckle. "And as you wish, I will tell the men about the killings, at the appointed moment."

So the plan was laid, the plan which meant reprieve for Erh Tan and a speedy shrift for the Devil's Bosun, with Coomassin looming ever larger to the north. Midmorning, indeed, should see the *Ta Ming* at anchor.

The island was irregular in shape, large in size, lying ten miles off the coast and the mouth of the Coomassin River. The town, such as it was, lay fronting the mainland, inside a long and narrow promontory. Within this headland lay the anchorage, gained by a narrow channel marked with sticks. Thus, as one fetched in from seaward, the town itself became revealed the very last thing, and what took the eye first was the promontory, with the impossible-looking channel.

Because of coral reefs between island and mainland, the approach was a bit tricky. Cairn sent Mr. Drift into the bow to keep an eye on the water ahead, for with the sun in the zenith coral is not readily discerned. He himself was scrutinizing the island and promontory through his binoculars, when Stella Tracey came to the bridge.

She was grave, unsmiling, her beautifully chiseled features

marked by grief. Cairn moved over to the port side, and she joined him there, inquiringly.

"Ali told me you must see me," she said.

Cairn nodded. "I'll have to give you a shock, I'm afraid. Couldn't tell you last night. You see, the mystery has vanished; I've got to the bottom of everything at last, and it's a bad business. You might take these glasses and pretend to be examining the island there."

She accepted the binoculars and lifted them to her eyes, training them on the island.

"Go ahead," she said quietly. "I don't think that anything you can tell me will prove much of a shock—just now."

"Maybe not." Cairn eyed the deck below. "Our friend Vandunk isn't what he seems. The real Vandunk was killed and chucked overboard the night we left port. This chap has impersonated him, put his own crew aboard here, and is going to raise merry hell if he's not blocked. I've thrown in with him, in order to block him more effectually."

"Well?" she said, no emotion in her voice. "Just who is he, then?"

"His name," said Cairn, "is Captain Patterson. Otherwise known as the Devil's Bosun."

THE WORDS might have meant nothing, for all the indication she showed. After a moment she lowered the glasses, her gaze fastened upon the island.

"Are you quite sure?"

"Quite."

"That would explain many things, then," she returned calmly. "Surely, everyone aboard is not with him?"

"Everyone except Ali and Erh Tan, yes. I don't know his purpose in regard to you, Miss Tracey. I hope to be able to block him at once, as soon as we cast anchor. If anything goes wrong, you must be prepared. He must not suspect me in any fashion; at all costs, he must think I'm tied to him."

"I see," she said. Then she stepped back a little from the ladder, looked down, and lowered the glasses. "Oh, Mynheer Vandunk! Coming up to enjoy the approach?"

The head of Vandunk appeared, then the rest of him. He had discarded shawl and mufflers. Now he was garbed in whites, a cap over his head. He smiled at the girl, flung Cairn a nod, and joined them.

"All well, Cap'n? Best take it cautiously; that's right. Devilish mean waters, I understand. No sign of that man Sabok?"

"He seems to have disappeared," Cairn rejoined, and moved away.

The island opened out, the channel appeared, like a gash of blue thrust into the tangled greenery of the island. A few native dugouts were scattered along the shores, and out between island and Celebes mainland fishing boats were at work.

No sign of the town appeared yet. Once the whole promontory had been a tangled mass of mangroves, whose roots blackened the whole shore. Now, for half its extent, it had been cleared away, so that the seaward portion showed a dazzle of white sand that ended smack against the wall of mangroves beyond. On this cleared portion, toward the tip, had been erected a fort, no doubt on the position of an earlier native fort. The place was all white in the sun, spick and span, the flag of the Netherlands drooping listlessly above, a few brass cannon glinting, a few sentinels in sight. The appearance of the ship seemed to create no commotion at all.

At half speed, she crept in toward the channel entrance. A gun boomed from the fort; Cairn nodded at the quartermaster, who ran up the colors. That channel was going to be a close business. It was deep enough, but narrow and curved like an elbow. Cairn, although he was really intent upon what would happen up forward at any instant now, could not but regard that channel nervously. He stood directing the helmsman as the ship swung. Beyond the channel stakes themselves, there was not above forty feet of water to either shore.

Suddenly, on the forward well deck, broke out a commotion. Voices were upraised, shrill and excited. Mr. Drift's voice emitted a roar from the bow. Cairn darted to the break of the bridge and looked down.

A Malay was nimbly running up the ladder, chattering excitedly at Vandunk. Down on the deck, half a dozen more of the men were circled about Ali. He stood there, kris in hand, teeth bared, his mocking tones driving at them all.

"Brethren of pigs! Aye, it was I who slew them, by Allah! Both of those men, and thereby gained paradise doubly, for both were Christians. Officers, aye; officers of swine like you—"

AT THE port side of the bridge, Cairn saw Vandunk move sharply, saw him reach hand to pocket, face ablaze. But shrewd old Ali had been watching that man also, and now leaped suddenly—leaped to the rail and stood poised there for an instant, and then was gone overside, down into the black waters, kris and all.

He had made it safely, with not an instant to spare.

Cairn darted back to the side of the helmsman, directed him sharply as the ship turned into the channel. From the rail, he caught the voice of Stella Tracey upraised in eager questioning. Vandunk made response.

"Confessed to murdering Lochaber and Andrews. The filthy dog! Yelled it at us and then ducked—"

Vandunk ran aft, pistol in hand, a fury of oaths on his lips. Cairn heard the pistol explode twice, but was not greatly worried. Inward exultation seized him. Ali had got clear away, would get ashore, would seek out the resident first thing and inform him of the whole business. The play had won, it had won!

The channel elbow opened. The ship slowly turned, made the bend perfectly. Cairn stepped out on the bridge and found Stella Tracey there. She turned and looked at him, and he read comprehension in her face. She nodded slightly; Ali had made the shore, then!

But, with this moment, sudden dismay smote Cairn. Out beyond the bend, signaling them where to anchor, lay a trim little launch with flag astern. A launch, with a strip of canvas over the stern for awning, and beneath it a man in whites, with a glint of gold braid showing. The resident in person; it could be no other.

A deep breath escaped Cairn. So much gambled, so little won! He had lost the game. Ali was somewhere far back at the channel. Here in the bight ahead, the half sheltered bight with poor holding ground, was the man he had gone ashore to find at such risk. Politely, eagerly, showing them anchorage and then coming aboard. Playing right into the hands of the Devil's Bosun.

The game was lost.

Vandunk came up, wiping his face, little shoe-button eyes glinting like jet. Cairn turned to him with a lift of brows.

"What's the rumpus about? I had to keep my attention on the channel—"

"That damned servant of yours," snapped Vandunk. "Confessed to murdering Lochaber and Andrews, then jumped and swam. I missed him, blast it! And I suspected the blighter all the time. Well, you can let that fat Chinese fool out now. We know the right man—and by the lord Harry, we'll get him! He's somewhere on this island."

Cairn whistled softly, as though in vast surprise.

CHAPTER VI

THE *Ta Ming* was at rest, her gangway down, the resident's launch hooked on to the landing below.

The resident himself was down in the cabin with Vandunk. Mr. Drift, with the ship's papers, had joined them; for the resident, it appeared, was also the port doctor, temporarily at least. That gentleman had recently died, leaving the resident with double duty.

Vandunk had quite succeeded in his impersonation.

With the ship securely moored as might be, Cairn got a bottle of Irish whiskey from his cabin and invited Mr. Drift to join him in a drink on the bridge, which Mr. Drift did with briskness and alacrity. So far as the ship was concerned, nothing much mattered now. En route, however, Cairn looked in on Erh Tan and told him he was free to act as he would, and left him again.

A drink felt good; Cairn needed it. He was well aware that now, whatever happened, it would be quite useless to take his story to the resident. Shrewd old Ali would no doubt conclude the same thing. The Devil's Bosun, having passed himself off as Vandunk was now impregnable. The resident would laugh at the truth with scorn, as well he might. So Cairn, leaving matters on the knees of the gods, discussed Irish whiskey very amiably with Mr. Drift, who had quite a taste for the liquor.

Midway of the drink, the resident came out on the lower deck, went to the rail, and volleyed Dutch at the sepoys in the launch. The latter cast off and headed for the wharf before the fort. Cairn gathered that an immediate search was ordered for Ali, who was to be run down at all costs.

One of the men, who had been exchanging talk with the sepoys, came to the bridge and reported to Mr. Drift, making it evident that Cairn was considered one of the crowd now. A week previously, the government steamer had been here and would not return for another three weeks. Two days before, a Chinese junk from Sandakan had put in and gone again. Nothing more was expected to happen. There was little sickness on the island.

Clearly, the Devil's Bosun had timed his visit with exactness. A government steamer might have interfered with his plans.

Over the mellow Irish, Cairn and Mr. Drift became very well acquainted, and discussed the town that lay outspread along the inner edge of the bight. Here was none of the terrible glaring cleanliness of the fort opposite, but a comfortable, unhurried,

ramshackle order of things. Houses on piles stood among the
mangrove roots at the shore, with two rickety old docks breaking their line, and many boats moored haphazard.

Back from these, in a luxuriant smother of foliage that broke
the sun's glare, stretched the town itself, or rather the village.
There was no order; the alleged streets were winding lanes. The
larger houses, the bazaars, each had its own kampong, with
plenty of room for trees, chickens, native servants, godowns. A
whitewashed but small mosque could be glimpsed.

F R O M O N E of the docks, a single broad avenue passed up
through the welter of houses and bazaars. Chinese traders were
here, as the white-and-blue posters smearing the front of certain
shops bore witness. On went the single avenue and ended up
on the hillside above the village in a huge gateway built of coral
blocks, where two guards in scarlet sarongs and uniforms were
visible. Behind this showed a massive growth of casuarina trees.

"That's the sultan's palace," and Mr. Drift jerked his thumb
at the gateway. "Can't see much of it from 'ere, though. I've 'eard
a lot about it," and he licked his lips, beneath his drooping
mustache, as though he had heard excellent things. Then his
eyes drove at Cairn. "What about shore leave, sir?"

"That's for Mynheer Vandunk to say."

Mr. Drift winked. "Right you are, sir. I see as we understand
each other. Liberal man, Vandunk is. Broad-minded, as the
saying goes, and you can count on 'is word any day. Well, sir,
'ere's your 'ealth!"

"Thanks," Cairn said drily, and emptied his glass.

A man summoned them down to Vandunk's cabin, to meet
the resident.

It was quite clear that everything had passed off radiantly,
for Vandunk was in a strangely affable manner. So was the
resident, thanks to the half-empty bottle of Hollands on the
table. He was a bald, worried man of forty, with bland and
ox-like eyes, a bovine air generally, and no great force. That he

was thankful to yield his responsibility here to Mynheer Vandunk, was quite plain.

"No, there is no trouble," he said, when the glasses had been filled anew. "The natives are cowed; Sultana Amina hates us bitterly, but is pleasant enough on the surface. We have had to shoot or deport a number of her advisors, and have formed a council of the younger rajas, men favorable to us. None the less, it is difficult to prevent her winning them over, for she is a woman of extraordinary personality and the people are devoted to her."

"I think," and Vandunk threw Cairn a glance, "that I'll be able to take care of the situation, so far as she's concerned. If she were removed, have you anyone who might take over the throne?"

"Oh, yes," and the resident brightened. "There is Lop Mansur, nephew of the old sultan, who has much influence and wealth. Unfortunately, I have only thirty soldiers here now. Many have died, and the invalids went with the steamer. A detachment will come by the next boat, but until then—"

"We have nearly twenty men aboard here," said Vandunk softly, "who can be turned into soldiers to fill the gap."

"Excellent," and the resident sipped his Hollands again. "Tell me, is there any truth in the rumor that the old sultan is not dead, but still living?"

Vandunk shrugged. He was not interested in the old sultan and knew nothing about him, and said as much, truthfully. Then he departed, after clearing away the glasses and bottle, to get Stella Tracey. The resident buttoned up his jacket, spruced up generally and received her with the greatest affability and sympathy.

"Unfortunately," he deplored, "we have no women here at all—that is, in the fort. Our soldiers are all natives, you comprehend. So I cannot well offer you quarters there. If you desire to remain here aboard the ship—"

"Of course I don't," said Miss Tracey with decision. "I'm

going ashore. Why can't I take a house in the town? Or stop at the palace, for that matter."

"The very thing!" exclaimed Vandunk quickly. He turned to the resident. "How can it be arranged?"

The resident smiled. "By this time, I imagine, the sultana is on her way to the town. She pretends to exert authority, you know; whenever a ship, even a junk, comes in, she comes down with guards and some of the council. We might wait till she comes, then go over to the wharf and present ourselves, eh? The matter will then arrange itself, beyond any doubt. And you, Mynheer Vandunk—will you accept quarters at the fort?"

"Thank you, no." Vandunk's bright, beady eyes were alive and glittering. "I'll go to the palace likewise, and exert a little authority of my own—"

"But it is not safe!" exclaimed the resident in dismay. "I cannot spare men to guard you there, mynheer. For you, it would not be safe at all; some of these natives are vindictive. And the sultana has her own guards—oh, a knife is so easily slipped in the back by these people!"

"In that case, I'll make it safe." Vandunk turned to Mr. Drift. "Have a boat broken out and at the gangway to take us ashore. Pick six men, Malays, not Chinese bloods, to act as my escort and to serve me; see that they're dressed fittingly. Serve out rifles and pistols to them."

"Right, sir—"

"Where'll you get the rifles and pistols?" put in Cairn amiably.

"From you." Vandunk chuckled. "You'll not mind turning over the keys to Mr. Drift, who'll keep the ship? You'll go with us to the palace, unless you object."

"I object to nothing," said Cairn with easy nonchalance. He produced his keys and tossed them across the table to Mr. Drift. "Worse luck, mister, that you must stay aboard!"

"If you'll excuse me, gentlemen," said Stella Tracey, "I'll get dressed more suitably and pack a few things."

CAIRN LEFT on the same errand. When he reached his own cabin, he found Erh Tan sitting there, mouthing a cheroot and awaiting him.

"Make yourself at home," he said. "What's up?"

"Nothing," said the plump young man. "I understand what has taken place and that I am in no danger. What shall I do?"

"Nothing," replied Cairn. "Stay here. I'm going ashore to the palace. You and Mr. Drift can take care of the ship."

Erh Tan looked alarmed at this prospect. "Mr. Drift? But—"

"Bah! You're in the hands of the Devil's Bosun, so make the best of it." Cairn began to dress in fresh garments. "It was my servant Ali who killed those two officers. I remember your esteemed relative once said that he was trying to teach you that the strongest forces in the world are often those which appear the weakest. Like my man Ali. So you've learned something. Make the most of it."

Perhaps his unconcealed contempt stung the plump young Celestial, for Erh Tan turned and departed in silence of dignity and rebuff. Cairn finished dressing, whistling merrily the while.

It was almost with wonder that he thought of his own fearful tension, a scant twenty-four hours previously. To be at sea, with the responsibility of a ship's master, is one thing; but that was all done with now. The land changed everything. Cairn was somewhat worried over Ali, a stranger in this island, hunted down for murder; but old Ali was no fool and could take care of himself.

Otherwise, come what might, things looked vastly different. Or at least, more hopeful. If Vandunk were put out of the way now, his scheme would fall to pieces. There was a wider horizon all around, as it were; things were no longer circumscribed by the narrow limits of a ship. Anything could happen here. One could breathe more easily, with freedom. So Mr. Drift was to keep the ship, eh? Cairn smiled at this, with a grim significance. It might well be that this move had saved Mr. Drift's life, at least for the present.

And then, of course, there was the Sultana Amina. With a laugh, Cairn pocketed the portrait of her.

One of the men came to summon him. Cairn hurried to the gangway and found Vandunk, the resident and Stella Tracey going down into the boat. Ashore, on the wharf at the end of the broad avenue, there was a brilliant splotch of color in the sunlight, and throngs of natives were gathering. Somewhere in town a brass gong, such as the Dyaks use to transmit messages over mountain and jungle, was thudding away with monotonous brazen voice.

The oarsmen gave way awkwardly, Cairn sitting with Stella Tracey, while Vandunk and the resident occupied the sternsheets. It was amusing to think how he would have resented this situation, a week earlier—he, so jealous of his authority as master! Vandunk had relegated him now to a mere escort for the English girl, and himself had taken over authority. The Devil's Bosun was certainly emerging.

BESIDES THE rowers, six of the men were crowded into the boat. Malays of the crew, now in bright sarongs, girded with pistols, rifles under arm. They grinned at Cairn, but beneath their grins he discerned unwonted arrogance. They, too, had now emerged from concealment. Deadly men these, deadly as the dead Sabok—and as readily killed. Cairn grinned back at them, and his gray eyes bit so hard that the brown men shifted glances uneasily. He, too, could cover menace with a grin.

"Does this sultana speak English?" Stella Tracey asked the resident. The latter mopped his bald brow and assented.

"Perfectly; she is English by birth, I think. No one is certain about that. No one knows except the old sultan, very likely. She speaks English and Dutch fluently. When she was a child, I understand, a missionary was here for some years, and gave her much instruction. Also, she has visited many cities, from Saigon to Manila. She is not a savage, if that is your meaning."

Not a savage, indeed! She stood out of the throng there on the wharf like a lily among rank grass. Cairn stared at her, rapt, forgetting himself; it was like seeing the reality of a dream. Among the bright sarongs and gold-braided jackets, the gay glitter of her guards, the fierce dark faces—he saw her alone.

The face was the same as that of the picture, yes; a little older, a little more lovely if anything, a little stronger. A slender oval face, with wide eyes, a hint of dignity, a touch of laughter; something undefinable about it all, impossible to describe. A look, a personality, fragile and ineffably delicate. Yet she was not fragile by any means.

Delicately slim and alluring in her dress of tussore silk, a parasol over her shoulder, a wide straw hat drooping above her brow—white, all white from head to foot. A girl just stepped from a Paris street, from Fifth Avenue, from the Esplanade. A sultana, the ruler of a Mohammedan island? Absurd! Utter nonsense. Her eyes found the unashamed, eager gaze of Cairn, and lingered on his face, half amused.

Then the resident mounted awkwardly, bowed to her, and began a formal introduction of the visitors. She nodded to Mynheer Vandunk, she gave Cairn another look—a straight, level look—then she held out her hand to Stella Tracey and a smile broke the lines of her features. A quick, friendly smile that warmed her dark eyes.

"Oh, I'm glad! I remember the name—it was your brother who was here, was it not? Why, what's wrong? What—"

"He died only yesterday," said Stella Tracey, flinching a trifle. One quick look, then Amina flung her arms about the other woman, impulsively.

"Oh, I'm sorry! How could I have known?" she cried. "Come; you're coming to the palace with me now, at once. These others may follow after us." A quick word to the guards, who closed around, and the two started off arm in arm. The resident grimaced awkwardly, then turned to the boat. He was out of it.

"The boat will take you back to the fort," said Vandunk, calling up his six guards. He said farewell to the resident, then took the arm of Cairn, and chuckled. "Well, my friend? You've seen her. Content?"

"Aye," said Cairn, and nodded. There was a flame in his gray eyes. Vandunk gestured to the guards and set forth with him. Officials crowded around in greeting; members of the council, rajas of the court. It was a tumultuous, vociferous throng that swept up the street in the wake of the two women.

THE GATES at last, where more scarlet-clad guards saluted. Little brown men, but armed with muskets, not rifles. The resident was obviously a cautious soul. Now the great casuarina trees, gently rustling in the breeze, slight as it was; "talking trees," the Malays called them. The sibilant whispers overhead were like the distant voices of a great throng, murmurous and filled with excitement.

Here were the palace grounds. Behind the edging of trees, carefully tended gardens surrounding the palace itself. A long, low building of white coral blocks, designed by some drunken beachcomber architect to judge by appearance. A building of vast extent, of arches and minarets, of plaster-work and the most rococo frills. Off to one side, a stables and other outbuildings and barracks for the guard.

Cairn drank it all in thirstily, not to say hungrily, for noon had come and gone and he had eaten nothing since early morning; but he had drunk plenty. Vandunk had fallen into deep converse with several gaudily dressed men of rank, members of the council by their talk; he paid no further heed to Cairn, but moved on with them, the six seamen sticking closely by him. Amina and Stella Tracey, somewhere in the van, had disappeared from sight.

Cairn lagged. In the cabin, he had pocketed a couple of Vandunk's cheroots. Now he paused to light one, then sauntered on toward the main palace entrance—a huge gateway, its arch adorned with Arabic inscriptions and colored tiles. Looking in, Cairn discovered that the palace was in reality a connected series of buildings, all fantastic in conception, erected around a vast courtyard aflame with flowers and gaudy blossoms and splashing with water from a dozen fountains, shaded here and there by enormous strips of colored silk awning. As a scene, it was gorgeous in the extreme, but not satisfying to a hungry stomach.

So far as Cairn could see, the others of his party had vanished from sight. He strode up to the guards, gave them affable greeting in Malay, and they gestured him on. Once beneath the arch, he found open doorways to right and left, and hesitated. Then, abruptly, a figure appeared before him. A strange figure, fantastic as the building.

"Ah, Captain!" boomed a deep voice. "So you have come!"

The English words met Cairn pleasantly. "Right," he said. "Where's Vandunk?"

"No matter, Captain, no matter," was the response. "I am glad that you let them come first; we may talk together. I am Chandra Das. Your agent talked with me at Sandakan; all is arranged. As steward of the palace and master of accounts, also B. A. from University of Calcutta, I have everything ready for you including luncheon with champagne. Follow me. In this place, all obey me. Excellency, I am your slave!"

Cairn blinked, but swallowed his astonishment. Chandra Das was a tall, burly, fat Baboo, greasily powerful in build, attired all in black with a sparkling white turban beautifully arranged. His black frock-coat displayed a heavy gold watch-chain crossing his vest. He salaamed to Cairn, then grinned to display solid gold teeth.

"Being acquainted with uniform of captain, also cap with oak leaves," he went on, "I make no mistake by advantage of education. I look in vain for anyone who must be Captain Patterson in escorted party. Now all is well. Accompany me, sir."

HE TURNED and led the way into the buildings at the right. Cairn followed, in careful silence. The name of Patterson tugged at him, broke his astonishment into swift comprehension. Things were unfolding and no mistake.

This fat but powerful Baboo was the steward of the sultanate, the man of affairs of the palace, the business head and brains of Coomassin. So much was clear. And the agent of the Devil's Bosun had arranged with Chandra Das for this very raid—the rascal was evidently behind the whole thing! Not knowing the Devil's Bosun personally, not knowing that Patterson was arriving in the guise of Mynheer Vandunk, he had greeted the uniform of Cairn with obvious recognition.

"We must talk fast," said Cairn suddenly, as he followed the other through vast rooms crowded with all manner of mechanical toys, cabinets, gilt furniture and similar gewgaws. "No time to waste."

Chandra Das waved his hand. "The others will not miss us," he said with unction. "Being a Hindu, I eat privately; I have arranged for us two. They will dine vastly with the sultana, but we shall taste the champagne of the old sultan, for I have the keys. Here, excellency, is my own apartment. It is yours, and all in it."

He threw open a door and salaamed again. Cairn stepped past him into a simply furnished living room, and beyond it a dining-room where the table glittered with silver and fine linen, and groaned with covered dishes. Wine coolers held champagne, and an open tantalus showed all manner of liquors and cigarettes.

Chandra Das carefully closed the doors, then rubbed his hands, enjoying Cairn's amazement.

"All is ready; no servants; we are alone in private," he declaimed grandly. "Sit, excellency. I make you welcome to my poor quarters."

Nothing loath, Cairn dropped into a chair; he was famished. Chandra Das grinned and made some jest about eating with a Christian, then sat down and began to serve food from the covered platters. A cork popped, and champagne bubbled.

"Look here!" exclaimed Cairn presently, forced to take the advantage lest the other do so. "You're well off here. Why bother to deal with my agent? I don't see just the point in your actions. What have you to gain from me?"

The Baboo chuckled, and washed down his curried fowl with a bumper of champagne.

"Did not your agent make it deaf, Captain?" he boomed. "Everything here is in my hands, but not for long. The Dutch support me, true, but this accursed girl on the throne hates me. She blames me for having delivered the old sultan into the power of the Dutch, an inconceivably wise thing for a poor Baboo to have done. Unless I abrogate my financial contract and retire, I much fear I should not live very long. So my contact with your agent. Your health, Captain!"

CAIRN SIPPED his champagne with relish. He was getting on to the hang of things now. This situation into which he had been so abruptly pitchforked was growing clear, and he meant to take advantage of it if he could.

Like many of his race in the eastern seas, Chandra Das was the business agent of Coomassin, and steward of the palace. All accounts passed through his hands. Obviously, he had helped betray Amina's father to the Dutch, hence his position was hardly secure.

"In other words," said Cairn, with a twinkle in his eye, "you prefer to leave here alive and well, and wealthy—eh?"

"Precisely, ornament of heaven!" boomed the Baboo. "My accounts in the safe in the business office are redundant with completeness. The property in the royal godowns is listed, tabulated, checked. The keys of the treasury I share with the sultana, but all there is likewise listed, from jewels to specie. Accounts payable from business agents in other ports amount to fifty thousand pounds English money, and I have very slyly arranged that they are payable to me as agent. Thus, there is no need to linger hereabouts, excellency."

"You're a wonder," said Cairn drily. His brain was racing. He knew that he must at all costs prevent a meeting between this man and Vandunk—at all costs! This fat rascal was the key to the whole plan of the Devil's Bosun.

"Are you aware," he asked, "that Mynheer Vandunk has come here with full powers?"

Chandra Das winked ponderously. "I presume so, and you are his ship captain, eh? Very clever, excellency. The first move, as I advised your agent, must be to clear that thrice-accursed girl from the path of mutual glory. In other words, place someone else on the throne. She is intolerable!"

"I bet she is," thought Cairn to himself, "especially to a fat pig like you!" But, aloud, he only murmured his complete agreement with the Baboo's astute plan, and allowed his plate to be heaped high anew and his glass filled. The champagne was magnificent.

"The agreement must be ratified, Captain Patterson," went on the deep voice. "To me, fifteen per centum of the whole thing, cash in hand out of the treasury, and a free passage away from here with you. That is understood?"

"Certainly," said Cairn, and grinned. "What assurance have you that I'll not cut your throat and make sure of your fifteen per centum?"

Chandra Das leaned back in his chair and heaved with hearty laughter until his gold watch-chain rolled again.

"Did not your agent make that clear, Captain? The best assurance in the world. The bills payable cannot be collected without me, or my signature as agent. We go and collect them at Sandakan, Brunei, and elsewhere. If you cut my throat, you would ineffably lose fifty thousand pounds English, which would be deplorable."

"Clever!" exclaimed Cairn cheerfully. "You're a sharp 'un, Chandra Das."

"Fairly so, if I may indulge in self-flattery," and the Baboo beamed. "As you know, the island is very rich, and the reefs along the north shores have been for years protected. The cream of two years' product is stored in the godowns; shell and bêche-de-mer and so forth. Everything is listed. The cargo alone should be worth a goodly ten thousand pounds English, according to my plentiful calculations."

"Not bad," said Cairn approvingly. Chandra Das shoved back his chair.

"If you permit, I will obtain the duplicate accounts from my private safe, with the orders I have made out to the guards of the godowns. Thus you will have no trouble in setting your men to work loading the goods aboard. One moment."

He rose and left the room.

Cairn sat for a moment in stupefaction at the whole thing. This man was working fast, and he was working to loot and destroy Coomassin. Something must be done, and done fast—but what?

Rising, Cairn went to the tantalus, helped himself to excellent cheroots, and lit one. He glanced about the room. On one wall hung a framed photograph of the sultana. Beside it hung another framed photograph. Cairn looked at this second one, and his jaw fell. He removed the cheroot and stared at the wall.

"Good lord!" he muttered. "It can't be—it just can't be—"

Utter and complete amazement gripped him. He had never suspected such a thing. Under the impact of the shock, he felt helpless, weak. And yet here was the one detail that cleared up everything, that banished the last of the whole mystery.

Chandra Das came back into the room. Then, at sight of Cairn's face, of the blazing gray eyes, he stopped short.

CHAPTER VII

"WHOSE IS that picture on the wall?" Cairn queried. "Beside that of the Sultana?"

"Oh, that is the old sultan," and Chandra Das chuckled disagreeably. "He wrote an inscription to me, as you can see, in

Arabic; hence, I kept it as a testimonial of my peculiar worth. Allow me to sit down, excellency, and get these papers in shape for your critical eye."

He plumped into a chair, cleared a space on the table, refilled the champagne glasses, and bent over his papers.

Cairn replaced the cheroot between his teeth and stared at the portrait of the old sultan. Despite the trappings of Malay royalty, the predominant thing about it was the pictured face— strong, filled with character, instinct with dignity and poise. No one who had seen those features could forget or mistake them.

A new wave of wonder swept over Cairn. He struggled to face the fact, to readjust himself to the truth. Now he understood perfectly why Lochaber and Andrews had been killed. He knew, in this moment, why Li Tock Lo had started a ball rolling, without knowing whither it would come to rest. He perceived the reason for the odd silence of Ali, and his more

singular lies regarding the past. He knew, in short, why Ali had taken service with him and had come to Coomassin.

For this picture revealed everything. The old sultan of Coomassin, deported and supposedly killed by the Dutch, had come home again.

The old sultan was Ali, his servant.

The strongest forces in the world are often those which appear the weakest—very true! Li Tock Lo must have had his

tongue in his cheek when he uttered those words, thought Cairn. That fat moon-faced Chinaman must have been behind Ali's escape from the Dutch all the time, must have arranged to send him back to Coomassin—why? No telling. How much had Li guessed, after all, about Vandunk? No telling. And why the devil had the ex-sultan been so desperately determined to get back here, where he certainly would not be safe? No telling, either; but the reason must have been a powerful one.

"And now," muttered Cairn, "there's the devil to pay all around!"

He turned and looked at the Baboo, whose fat neck creased over his collar as he sat checking the papers. This poisonous spider had betrayed his master, was betraying the sultana, was deliberately arranging everything—had even brought the Devil's Bosun here! And now, if he met the real Patterson, the result might be frightful to all concerned. His entirely natural error in mistaking Cairn for the other, must be put to advantage—instantly. There was no other way, there was no alternative. It was the survival of the fittest; the old law of the sea brought ashore.

A gurgle broke from Chandra Das. He slumped forward on the table, sending a glass crashing, and lay there, without a word. The blow had taken him squarely across the base of the brain, where his fat neck bulged; a blow bad enough when delivered with a fist, as every boxer knows, but tenfold more deadly when delivered with the flat edge of the hand—as every Japanese knows. Then, and then only, an acute paralysis is induced, which may last an hour or more.

Cairn rubbed his hand; the blow had hurt. He could take no chances, for this rascally Baboo was powerful. Well indeed that he had taken no chances, as he perceived a moment later when he frisked the paralyzed and unconscious figure. An armpit holster and pistol, which he transferred to himself, and a deadly long knife, which he pitched on the table.

Stuffed pockets. Money, packets of it; all kinds of paper money, bills of accounts, rouleaux of gold, packets of gems. Graft or outright theft, beyond any doubt. Cairn pocketed the lot, then looked around thoughtfully.

A large closet in one corner caught his eye. He went to it, found it locked. From the pockets of Chandra Das he had taken a large bunch of keys. Patiently he tried these, until one fitted

and the door swung open. Here, where it would be least suspected, was a species of gun room; rifles and shotguns neatly
racked, pistols, long krisses and spears, boxes of ammunition.
Weapons, no doubt, hidden away from the Dutch and left in
the care of the Baboo.

CAIRN CLEARED them back into a pile, making room.
He went to the table and fell to work with napkins and strips
of the linen cloth, presently he had Chandra Das uncomfortably
but safely trussed, with a linen gag in his mouth that would
stop any coherent utterance. Then, with much effort, he dragged
his victim over to the closet, intending to deposit him there for
later reference.

He was at the doorway, in the very act of bundling Chandra
Das inside, when a sharp gasp, an intake of breath, caught his
attention. Cairn straightened up, just in time to see a moving
shape—a Malay leaping for him, uttering a shrill cry, kris all
aflame and striking in for him. A servant of the Baboo, no
doubt.

Evasion was impossible. No time for a gun. The darting figure
was upon him all in an instant. Cairn struck the knife-arm
aside; with the impact, both men went down in a heap above
the figure of Chandra Das, the wild cry of outraged ferocity
ringing high. In that confined space their two figures thrashed
about frantically.

Cairn had a grip on the slender man, but the muscles under
his hand were as corded steel. The Malay whipped back and
forth; it was like holding a striking snake by the tail. The kris
drove in and out, Cairn somehow knocking it aside—then the
weapon thudded home. But Cairn's iron fingers had found their
mark; they closed about the brown throat, closed with a ferocity, a savage outburst of energy that sank them into the flesh.

Half-crouched, Cairn kept his grip grimly, while the lithe
figure slowly grew limp and relaxed. It was hanging in his hands,
like a doll. He came erect, but the brown body jerked at him,
as though anchored to the floor. Cairn blinked the sweat from

his eyes and peered down, surprised. A low exclamation burst from him.

The kris, still gripped by the dead brown hand, was buried to the very hilt in the body of Chandra Das. Driven in, through throat and breast—a chance stroke that had found deadly entry.

Cairn dropped the lolling-tongued thing from which he had squeezed the life. A shudder passed through him; he stepped from the closet and, after an effort, slammed the door and locked it. He went to the table, seized the champagne bottle, and gulped down some of the liquid. His head cleared.

The brown devil had not missed him by much. His coat pocket was ripped. The kris had struck against the flat automatic pistol there and glanced—perhaps for its fatal thrust. Almost mechanically, he reached out and took the papers Chandra Das had fetched from his safe. Glancing over them, Cairn thrust them into a pocket.

"And now what?" he thought. "Better get in touch with the sultana right off. If Vandunk is in the notion of quick action, as this Baboo indicated, we've no time to lose. What the devil! To think of old Ali being the ex-sultan, and lying like a good one about his past!"

He glanced out at the garden. No, not there; his way lay into the palace. He turned, stepped out of the dining-room, and closed the door behind him.

PRESENTLY HE was out of the Baboo's apartment entirely. Then he halted. Which way? A corridor was before him; had he come from right or left? He could not recall, but it would make little difference. With a shrug, he turned to the right. His coat bulged. His pockets were filled, and besides his Webley he now had an automatic under his armpit. Best find the sultana at once, turn over his loot to her, and consult as to some course of action. Stella Tracey must have warned her by this time, of course.

There was the Devil's Bosun to think about, also. Vandunk

was not going to let his chief helper disappear for long, and not do something about it.

Cairn strode on down the passage; it seemed interminable. Then, ahead of him came an archway and sunlight, filtering down through greenery. This was not the way he had come, he now knew definitely, but he went on. Somewhere he would come out on the central patio, or reach one of the guards to direct him.

In the archway, he paused in dismay. A wall rose to right and left, tree branches leaning over them. Directly ahead, six feet away, were a door and another of the buildings that comprised the palace cluster. With a shrug, he passed on, tried the door, and after a hard pull it opened. Long disused, apparently.

Another corridor, with a sharp turn ahead. The sound of splashing fountains reached him; good! He must be near the central court. At the turn, a heavy curtain barred his way. He heaved it aside, unsuspecting—and went headlong.

Steps, unexpected; polished marble steps. He had a swift vision of them as he lurched downward and lost balance. He had a swift vision of a tiled bath where women were disporting themselves, brown women and girls; a swift, horrified vision. Their startled outcry rang in his ears. A glimpse of luxury; rich textiles, birds in cages, divans and cushions. All this in one flashing split second. Then he was falling, trying frantically to right himself—crash!

A thunder of stars as he went head-on against a pillar, and darkness.

Wakening came with a sense of oppression, of constriction, for which he could not account. He tried to move, and could not. His head felt as though gripped in a vise.

Then memory flashed into him. He had somehow blundered into the women's quarter of the palace; worse yet, into the women's very bath! Sacrilege of sacrilege, at least from a Mohammedan viewpoint. Amina would not be living in a harem, of course, but this was undoubtedly the harem of the ex-sultan.

Cairn's head throbbed. Filaments of daylight reached his eyes, but he could see nothing; a cloth was wrapped about his head and eyes, probably a blindfold rather than a bandage for his cracked pate. And his mouth was held in a relentless clasp. A gag, most efficient, that irked cruelly. He was sitting in a chair of some kind, to which his wrists and ankles were bound fast.

There was a fluttering of voices and soft laughter about him. Women! He must still be in the same place, then; he could hear water splashing close by. He tried to speak, and could utter only a growling groan.

More laughter. A pad-pad of bare feet on the marble, and strong perfumes assailed his nostrils. Women were all around; their fingers touched him mockingly. Panic laid hold on him. Struggling, Cairn tore at his bonds, all in vain, and relaxed again, breathing hard, muttering curses that came forth only as dull harsh sounds.

He winced, as a hand touched his sore head. It slid down and caressed his cheek. A voice spoke, with muffled laughter, in Malay.

"So the handsome Christian captain desired to look upon the women of the palace! And in his eagerness, he flung himself among them. Are there no infidel women, then, to slake his fury with kisses? Why should he seek out the women of true believers?"

"All Christians are curious, my daughter," croaked an older voice, with a hideous cackle of mirth. "Whether they be of Dutch or of other nations, they cannot stay away from women, but seek them out at all cost. Take my advice and call the guards, that they may slay this man quickly."

"No, no!" There was a little chorus of protest. Cairn realized there must be a number of women around him. Sweat started on his forehead. He comprehended now that these women must have tied him up while he was knocked out.

"Touch not his money or weapons," spoke out a stronger, more authoritative voice. "Yet he must not go unpunished. Since his eyes have offended, let them pay for the insult. Prick them out with needles, then turn him loose into the garden."

Another chorus, this time of eager affirmation. Beneath the mirth in these soft voices lay an undertone of cruelty, like that of most savage nations. Primitive mirth was based on cruelty. But now arose discussion, as Cairn sat there helpless and sweated in stark fear.

"Not yet, not yet!" sounded a voice almost at his ear. "Time enough for that when the moment comes. Look at me, infidel; am I not beautiful? Think how many men would give all that they have to sit where you sit, and behold me!"

"Bah! She lies, the cat!" chipped in another voice, amid a burst of laughter. "Not a drop of henna anywhere, and if she hasn't thirty years and ten squealing brats, may I be married to a Chinaman! Look at this paragon of beauty who addresses you, who lays at your feet all the loveliness that has made her famous through the world. I sigh for you, handsome infidel, and I embrace you!"

S O F T   F I N G E R S flicked along his cheek. Whatever that embrace was, the gay chime of laughter that arose showed it did not lack in humor. Cairn's panic deepened into actual horror. These women, he knew well, were capable of anything. He had laid himself open to any punishment they might inflict, and if it stopped at merely blinding him, he might well prove lucky.

"Perhaps he came here not to see us, but to bathe!" suggested someone. "Throw him into the pool and see if he can swim, chair and all—"

Various suggestions followed, none of them being put into effect. Savagely Cairn bit at his gag, tried to eject it from his mouth. A word of explanation, and at least he could force them to bring the sultana. But his efforts were useless. Irony of fate! He had condemned Chandra Das to the very situation in which he now found himself, except for the cruel mockery around him.

"Bring needles, bring needles!" came that same voice of authority which had first mentioned the blinding. "What sport is there in jeering at an elephant in a pit? Let him go forth blinded by the sight of our beauty!"

Cairn began to sweat afresh, for in this voice was a horrible earnestness and cold cruelty that banished all thought of jesting. The woman meant her words.

"First let him speak," said someone. "I have heard that the talk of Christians is like the rustling of leaves—"

"No, keep him as he is," came the quick retort. "I remember that in the time of the Sultan Ali a *hakim*, a doctor, came among us and brought with him an official. And what happened to this man, who dared to look upon the women of the harem? He was cut down by the guards and sliced with knives. But now we are ruled by a woman, and she dare not act so shrewdly. So let this infidel not cry out, lest the guards spoil our fun."

Cairn tried to wrench his clammy hands through the lashings, in vain. His agitation caused fresh laughter; the women pressed about him closely, mocking him, jeering at him, heaping him with insults. Their mood was changing from amusement to cruelty. One of them sank her fingers in his throat, until others tore her away.

"Here are needles!" went up a panting cry, and the pad-pad of running feet. "Give me one eye, for my trouble in getting them! Uncover his eye, quickly!"

Excitement shrilled the voices. Cairn could hear a wild squabble over the needles, and cold terror seized upon him. These she-devils were in earnest, all right. Harem beauties! He groaned, and at his gulping sound they broke into delighted cries. They comprehended his torment and enjoyed it.

An overwhelming reek of perfume. He was aware of a woman beside him, touching him, baring his throat.

"Feel, infidel, feel!" A needle jabbed into his chest, and he winced. "Next in your pretty eyes, that dared so greatly and yet failed so far! Too eager, Christian, for your own good—"

A hand caught at the bandage about his eyes. Then, as he

resigned himself to the horror of it, fell a sudden startled silence. He heard a quick gasping of breath, felt the woman beside him withdraw.

"What is this?" rose a voice—a new voice, startled, angry, dominant. "A man, here in the bath? And you, sisters of devils— oh!" The cry was swift and shrill. "Out of here! Instantly! Begone!"

There was a movement, an outburst of voices in shrill explanation and excuse. A sudden rush, and he heard the voice of Stella Tracey.

"Cairn—Captain Cairn! Here he is now—"Then she was at his side. She caught the blindfold and tore it away. He saw her bending over him; and behind her, standing on steps above the bath, the sultana. The others were gone, with a chittering burst of indignant lessening voices.

The gag yielded. Cairn gulped for air, tried to work his jaws, and failed. For the moment he was helpless to speak. Stella Tracey worked at his bonds.

"How did it happen? How did you get here?" she exclaimed quickly. "We missed you. They are searching everywhere for you now—no one had seen you in the palace. There; that's better."

She knelt and fell to work at his ankles. Above her stooped shoulders, Cairn met the gaze of Amina the sultana; an inquiring, half angry, half amused look. A little color rose in her lovely features.

"Just got here—in time," he mumbled, as speech returned. "Can't blame 'em. I fell in here—tumbled down the stairs and hit my head. They didn't understand."

Amina broke into a smile. "Naturally they wouldn't," she said in flawless English. "In fact, Captain Cairn, you'd have a good deal of trouble making anyone understand, I imagine."

"Not you," said Cairn. His feet, were free now. He stood up. "Thanks, Miss Tracey." He caught her hand, helped her to her feet. Then his gaze went again to Amina, standing there and regarding him. "No, not you, Sultana," he said awkwardly. "I can make you savvy quick, enough—what do I call you? Royal Highness or something?"

She broke into a laugh. "Since my birth-name happens to be Talbot, I suppose I'm Miss Talbot. Or Amina, as you please. There certainly need be no formality among friends. Especially under the circumstances. Miss Tracey has told me the whole thing."

"You mean—"

"The truth about Mynheer Vandunk." A swift flash of anger lightened her dark eyes. "I don't know what to do, whom to reach. The resident distrusts me. My guards are faithful, but they can do little against soldiers. And this—this pig has taken over part of the palace with his men! They have rifles."

"Well, we can't stand here talking all day," said Cairn. He was rapidly becoming himself once more. "I've got my pockets filled with stuff belonging to you, and want to get rid of it; money and papers and so on. I was trying to find you when I stumbled in here. Your friend Chandra Das was in cahoots with the Devil's Bosun—"

HE TOOK a step, and staggered. His head whirled. Putting up a hand, he discovered an egg-shaped bump over one ear. Stella Tracey caught his arm quickly.

"Where can we go, Amina?" she exclaimed. "Something must have happened that we don't know—we can't stay here—"

"Come into my apartment," said the sultana quietly. "I'll keep everyone out, even my own maids. How lucky that I wanted to show you the baths! Bring him. I'll go ahead and make sure everything is clear."

She turned and went up the steps. Cairn patted Stella Tracey's arm.

"I'm quite all right, thanks—just dizzy for a minute," he said abruptly. "This bump unsettled me. Come along."

What with one thing and another, time had elapsed since their arrival at the palace. From the passage into which they turned, he had a glimpse of the gardens through latticed windows, and perceived that the sun was westering fast.

"You mean to say nobody knows where I am?" he asked. Miss Tracey nodded.

"Precisely. Everything seems to have gone to pieces here; Vandunk has taken one of the palace buildings and is receiving some of the nobles. The poor girl there," and she motioned to Amina, ahead of them, "doesn't know what to make of it. Or rather, she didn't, until I told her everything."

"You don't know everything," Cairn said grimly.

The sultana held a door open, then shut and bolted it behind them.

Cairn was astonished. Even after his sight of Amina on the wharf, he none the less associated her with oriental luxury and the pomp of position; the very name of "sultana" suggested this.

Here in her apartment, however, everything fell away. Gone were the last vestiges of Coomassin; here was a small suite of rooms as refreshingly European as a Park Avenue lodging. Curtains at the windows, rugs and furniture of French extraction, shaded lamps, a writing desk, pictures on the walls—he swallowed hard, accepted the chair offered him, and found himself face to face with Amina Talbot. The sultana was gone.

"If you don't mind," said Stella Tracey, at the door of the adjoining room, "I'll bathe and change my gown."

"The room's yours, my dear," said Amina, and reached for a cigarette.

CAIRN COLLECTED himself with an effort, held match for her, accepted a smoke himself. He needed it. He could not believe that he was on the island of Coomassin. Every moment seemed to present everything in a new and unexpected light; the shifting of scenes was rapid and totally different, like the changing scenes in a kaleidoscope. From that murderous affair with the Baboo, into the ghastly humor of the women's bath, and now—this!

Strangest of all, the woman before him, smiling slightly as

she regarded him, a warm friendliness in her eyes, entirely at her ease. All crisis was very distant and far away. It was like being in a dream. He had thought her aping European ways, perhaps, but she was not; she was of his own people, his own class, his own blood. She must have read the expression in his eyes, for she broke into a silvery laugh.

"You are so astonished at finding things—like this? Come, Captain Cairn; we're realities, you know. It's only in a cinema that you'd find a gorgeous sultana draped in ropes of pearls and ordering ranks of slaves about."

"Cinema! That word spoils the charm," and Cairn relaxed, his gray eyes twinkling. "If you'd said moving picture, I'd have taken you for an American on the spot. No; you're far more lovely than any painted screen sultana. I didn't think it could be true."

"What?" she questioned, with an inquiring lift of her brows. Cairn fell into swift confusion and wakened to where he was, why he had come. He began to pile money and gems and papers out on the table, emptied his pockets, while she stared wide-eyed.

"Whatever is all this? Where did you get it?"

"Yours," said Cairn. "All yours, Miss Talbot. Here are the papers regarding the bills payable elsewhere—I got all this from Chandra Das, you know."

"And this, too?" She leaned forward, pressed out her cigarette in an ash tray, and picked up a square of paper that had fallen out with the other stuff. A photograph. She looked at it in astonishment, then at Cairn. "My picture! Did Chandra Das have it?"

"No." Cairn flushed. "No. I got it—in Surabaya. That's what I didn't believe was true—that anyone could look like it. But never mind all that, Miss Talbot. You've got to buck up and act," he said earnestly. "You see, Chandra Das let out a good deal of information before he died. He thought that I was the Devil's Bo—"

"What's that? Did you say Chandra is dead?" She started up, a sudden spark in her eyes. "It's impossible! Tell me quickly."

"Well, give me a chance." Cairn leaned back. "That's why I got lost. He met me and took me for Cap'n Patterson—" and in few words, he related the tragic mistake made by the Baboo, and its consequences. She listened with kindling eyes and animated features; swift energy leaped into her expression, and her voice rang out upon the room when he had finished.

"Dead! That unspeakable rascal, dead! And I have longed for the conscience to order his death—I could not do it. I am not one of these people whom I rule. And now he is dead! Well, he deserved it."

The spark died. Her clenched hands fell in her lap.

"But what can I do?" she exclaimed, helplessly. "Miss Tracey told me about this man who pretends to be Vandunk. What can I do? My people are scattered over the island; they have no arms, they are cowed. Half of the rajas, even of the council, plot against me and hate me because I'm not of their race. I know not whom to trust among my own guards. The Dutch resident—ah, the fat pig! He has no intelligence."

"Well," said Cairn, "you can't sit and wring your hands, that's sure. One good thing has been done; the Devil's Bosun has lost his friend and ally the Baboo. I'd say, put a bullet into Vandunk first thing. Show me where he is, and I'll take care of him."

Pallor grew in her oval face as she met his incisive eyes.

"No," she said in a low voice. "He has taken the corner building, at the end of the palace. You do not understand. My father—rather, the old sultan—built it and it is like a fort in itself. He has his own men from the ship there, and a number of my guards—don't you see? Many of the council support him already. Even before we sat down to the table, he had won them over. They know that I am to be deposed. That is all they want. You cannot reach him, cannot—"

Her voice died out in despair. It was as though she suddenly beheld the gulf yawning beneath her; the situation in which she was utterly helpless and unable to act. Despair indeed, and panic. To struggle was hopeless.

I N T H E silence, the adjoining door opened and Stella Tracey appeared, fresh and glowing. She stopped short at sight of their expressions.

"What? Lost in gloom?" she exclaimed. "Tell me about it. Captain Cairn, can't you do any better than cast a shadow over our hostess?"

"He's tried hard enough to do better," and Amina Talbot smiled faintly. "I'm afraid it just won't work. Sit down and listen to it. Tell me what to do."

Stella Tracey, cool and incisive, joined them; she seemed more frigid, more coldly aloof than ever, as Cairn outlined the situation. Her blue eyes dwelt upon him with a chill reserve. He could not understand her attitude. Yet there was a strength in her very coolness, a quiet poise, a comprehension, that was heartening.

Then, abruptly, Cairn checked himself. For the first time, he recollected Ali, and the amazing recognition of the old sultan in his servant. And like a thunderbolt, the thought struck him aghast: this man, deposed and exiled and prisoned by the Dutch, certainly would not have gone to the resident with any warning against Vandunk. Ali would not have dared risk recognition. Whatever his purpose in wanting to regain the island of Coomassin—perhaps sheer homesickness—Ali would never have carried this warning. Even had he been able to reach the resident, he would not have done so.

"The old rascal put it over on me!" thought Cairn.

He was about to tell the sultana about her adopted father, when she broke out into weary utterance.

"Oh, what does it all matter! Let them depose me. Let them have their way. I don't want to stay here. I've longed to leave this place for ever. There was only one person I ever knew who loved me and whom I loved; whom I could respect, upon whom I could depend utterly. And him they took away in chains. Let them loot and fight over the loot. What does it matter? For me, there can only be escape—if that."

"Perhaps," said Cairn slowly, "they would not be satisfied to have you escape. Perhaps they mean to make sure of you—by marriage. Perhaps Vandunk hopes to get money by placing a certain Lop Mansur on the throne in your place; perhaps he has even offered your hand in marriage to someone else."

"Lop Mansur—that beast!" cried out the sultana. Her head lifted, her nostrils dilated; a flash shone again in her eyes. "Give me—in marriage? Sell me like a chattel, like a Chinese woman? Oh, if my father Ali were here—"

"He is here," said Cairn shortly. Her eyes widened upon him. She caught her breath sharply.

"Here? You must be out of your senses! He is a prisoner in Java—"

"He's here," Cairn repeated, and smiled. He glanced at the wondering Stella Tracey. "My servant, Ali. There was a picture of the former sultan in Chandra's room; I recognized him instantly."

Suddenly Amina Talbot was beside him, clutching his hands, looking into his face; her nearness, the pressure of her fingers, the eager radiance illumining her features, was overpowering. Cairn felt himself shaken, trembling.

"Here, and alive? And you brought him? Oh, my friend!" Her voice lingered on the word like a softly echoing bell. "You do not know what this means. Now I am alive again, now I am myself, life is worth living, worth fighting for—"

A sudden sharp hammering at the door broke in upon her, silenced her. She turned and called inquiringly. A voice made response in Malay, respectful, subservient. Cairn caught the words.

In two hours there would be a meeting of the council. Her presence was requested. The Dutch controller, Mynheer Vandunk, and the resident were to be present. In the hall of audience, in two hours. That was all.

Silence fell upon the room. Cairn became aware that the sun had disappeared, that dusk was gathering outside. The sultana was staring at him, her face aglow with pride and anger; no more helplessness, no more wringing of hands. The crisis was upon her, and she was rising to it.

"So you were right! They will strike—good! I am still the sultana," she exclaimed with energy. Then she broke into a laugh. "Two hours! Until then, my friends, let us make the most of our time."

"I think I'll go out for a walk about the place," said Stella Tracey in her aloof way, and Cairn felt the touch of her eyes, blue and icy, as they passed over him and over the sultana with unspoken message. She walked to the door, unbarred it, and was gone. Cairn frowned a little, wondering at her manner. Then he forgot her again.

Vandunk was not delaying his stroke!

CHAPTER VIII

AMINA TALBOT went into another room and closed the door. Cairn heard the sound of a gong, heard her voice giving directions; presently she came back, pulled the curtains, and lit softly glowing lamps.

It was like a dream to Cairn, all of it. She was like a dream-fairy come to life. Caught unguarded in this unsuspected environment, Cairn had been awkward and embarrassed, self-conscious. This, perhaps, was why Stella Tracey had left them alone.

Now, in the lamplight, everything was different; once more the scene had shifted again, and Cairn came to his feet, lit a cigarette, suddenly found himself free of all restraint. They two were together, and the world of Coomassin was shut out.

"Tell me about him—my adopted father," said Amina softly. "How did he come here? Where is he now?"

Cairn told her. He spoke crisply, curtly, laid bare everything in few words. Ali had swum ashore, was perhaps hiding somewhere. Smiling, she shook her head.

"You don't know him. To many of the natives he is their great hero; he will have found friends and shelter ere this. It was to find me, to protect me, that he came back here. He had no children—those he had, are dead. That was why he adopted me when I was a child. Well, we shall see! I don't know what to expect, what to think."

"Still hesitant?" snapped Cairn. "Still wringing your hands?"

"No," she said gravely, looking at him. Just the one word; it spoke volumes. Her face lit up, strangely radiant. They were standing close together, beside the desk and the lamp there. "Be careful! You're impatient, energetic, reckless. You must be careful."

"Why?" demanded Cairn, thrilled by the low timbre of her voice, by the singular beauty of her look. Something seemed drawing them together; he was conscious of her compellent personality, of her warm liking, of her friendship.

"Why? Because you have come into this place like a breath of vigorous and clean life," she exclaimed. "You, and this English woman. She looks strong; she is really weak. But you have strength for all."

"Stella Tracey weak?" Cairn laughed harshly. "Not she! But you—you—"

He checked his words, only to find her eyes bidding him on. He yielded.

"Call it madness, insolence, anything you like," he broke out, facing her frankly, looking into her eyes, a rugged earnestness in his attitude and words. "You showed me a new horizon before I ever saw you, Amina. Your picture, the look in your eyes—bah! Words are too small for it all. It's a big thing, a tremendous thing."

Courage grew in her steady gaze. Color climbed her cheek.

"That's why, perhaps, I told you just now to be careful," she said softly. "Because I don't want you to go under—poison, a stab in the back, a bullet. I know these people of mine. I know this place. I abhor it and them; all except one man. And you. When I looked down from the wharf into the boat, and met your eyes, it was as though the world turned over. Should I say such things to you, a stranger? But you're not a stranger, my friend."

"No, thank heaven!" said Cairn, a little hoarsely.

SILENCE FELL upon them. He reached out and she gave him her hand. Cairn knew his pulses were throbbing, a hammer was pounding at his temples, a joyous eagerness flooding through his veins. She was big enough to be herself. Nothing petty in all this, nothing sordid or small; no talk of love, though it underlay everything. Or was it love that had drawn them so, that compelled them now to open speaking, frank words?

Understanding, rather.

She was smiling, trembling a little; he released her fingers, reverently.

"My dear, my dear, there is so much we do not need to say!" he exclaimed under his breath. A short, sharp knock at the door, and the voice of Stella Tracey reached them. Cairn went to the door and opened it, shooting the bolt again when Miss Tracey had entered. From another room came the chiming of a gong.

"Just in time!" cried Amina brightly, catching Stella's hands in her own, putting an arm about her. "Supper is ready; I told them to serve it and summon me, and stay out. They do not know Captain Cairn is here."

"They must not know," said Stella Tracey quietly. "I met the resident, coming to dine with Vandunk and some of your council. He was much worried. He said the town is being searched—you're supposed to have disappeared while drunk, Captain Cairn. What about those women of yours, Amina? Will they talk?"

"Of course, in time," said Amina coolly. "Let them! Tomorrow is another day. Come along; eat, drink and be merry! You said nothing to the resident about Vandunk?"

Stella Tracey colored. "Yes, I did. He wouldn't listen to me. No sooner had I blurted out that Vandunk was an impostor, than he waved his hands, rolled his eyes, and turned his back on me. He muttered something about sun-struck Englanders. He was worried, wildly nervous, and I think had been drinking. He had some soldiers with him."

"Yes, he always drinks toward evening," said Amina quietly. "Schnapps. He drinks heavily and in the morning has terrible headaches. He is a perfect pig, that man."

"And now I suppose the fat's in the fire," Miss Tracey observed, her voice all drooping. "He'll tell Vandunk what I said."

"What of it?" Amina Talbot laughed gaily and pressed the shoulders of the other woman. "Let it pass; they'll do no more than keep us under guard. Come along! We'll talk about it at the table. I have a plan. You see, I'm not wringing my hands any longer!"

And she darted a gay glance at Cairn, as she flung open the door.

A dining-room was disclosed, the table laid for two in tasteful elegance; none of the Baboo's vulgar display was here visible. There was no wine. Sandwiches, salad, coffee; nothing else.

"First, about you." Amina turned to Cairn, decision in her manner. "Can you rejoin Vandunk?"

"Certainly. If I don't delay too long about it."

"You'd be more help there than here. I can plan nothing definitely until I get in touch with my adopted father; Ali will have something in mind."

"Force?" queried Cairn. She shook her head.

"Not against the Dutch. We have not many people; the plague swept away numbers, others were killed in the revolt. They are cowed, afraid. The guns of the fort can sweep the town. Would there be any way of leaving here altogether? On your ship?"

"Not without a crew."

Her eyes flashed. "Suppose I could provide a crew? Our

people are seamen. Many of them have served in ships like yours."

"Then it would be possible—in an emergency. But the fort could sink us in five minutes. We couldn't leave the harbor without permission of the resident."

"Understood, then," she said coolly. "Go back to Vandunk. I'll attend the council and see what he intends. I can communicate with you later—perhaps in the morning. There are two of the servants on whom I can depend absolutely. It may be that we'll simply take one of the native boats and head for the mainland."

"Depends on Ali, eh? All right; count on me. What about Miss Tracey?"

"She'll remain here, with me. Do nothing rash; await word from me. Agreed?"

Cairn shrugged. "I suppose so. I still think the best plan is to slap a bullet into Vandunk—"

"No, no!" she broke in quickly. "Don't you see? It would mean a massacre. The resident—oh, it would be terrible! And these Malays are my people. I must protect them, look out for them."

"Have it your own way, then. But there's bound to be a showdown. This Devil's Bosun knows the value of a bold, quick stroke. Look out, or he'll have everything right where he wants it! Now tell me how to reach the building he's in. No time to lose if I'm to rejoin him."

She swiftly sketched the position indicated. Cairn nodded, rose, and put out his hand to Stella Tracey. As he met her blue eyes, he was astonished; for in their depths he read a lurking fear, an apprehension. Was it possible that Amina had judged her aright? Her brother's death, perhaps, had broken down her frigid reserve.

"Buck up," he said cheerfully. "You still have your Webley?"

She nodded, smiled a little, and he turned to the door. Amina came to let him out. She met his eyes for a moment, searchingly; her fingers closed on his.

"Good-by; good luck," she breathed. "If you should come to the council—remember! Do nothing rash. Whatever happens, be careful; you're the one hope."

Then he was outside, and the door was barred again.

The one hope! Cairn swore softly to himself. She was past all comprehension. Give him his own way, and this affair would be ended at a blow—if nothing happened to him. He suddenly perceived that this was exactly what was in her mind. She dared not jeopardize him. She must wait, get in touch with Ali, leave Cairn as a sort of last anchor for emergencies. She could not risk anything going wrong. At the worst, he could get her and Ali away from here in a native boat. Perhaps this was what lay in her mind.

Down a passage, to the left, burned a lamp; two guards were standing there in talk. Cairn turned right, as she had told him, and followed the corridor. Another lamp, two more guards ahead; but first the door she had indicated. It opened to his hand. He stepped into darkness, closed the door, and struck a match.

Yes, this was the place. The administrative office of the sultanate, with its desks and chairs and files. And beyond, the windows opening on the central patio.

BEHIND, IN the corridor Cairn had just left, the two guards came quickly, stealthily. They paused at the door which he had just closed; they listened, heard his swift, firm steps. Booted leather rings on coral blocks. They heard the creak of a window swung open. They looked at one another, then they turned and hurriedly departed.

The great courtyard, or rather the paths that crisscrossed among the flowers and orange-trees, were lighted by tall post-lanterns. Cairn encountered many figures, natives of rank, servants, guards. Some stopped to stare after him amazedly, others paid him no attention. His white uniform, of course, marked him out with startling clarity, his height made him doubly conspicuous.

Off in the jungle, gongs were beating monotonously, thud-dingly, sending thin brazen shudders of vibrance across the night. There was no moon, but the stars blazed brightly. From somewhere about the palace came the strident voice of a radio, and the soft excited flutterings of women's voices. The casua-rina trees roundabout were stirred by a low breeze, so that multitudes of people seemed talking distantly. Somehow, a vague but decided oppression seized upon Cairn; a sense of expectancy, of waiting, of near crisis at hand. He swore under his breath at it, and went on.

The building was not hard to find. It was ablaze with light, and high lanterns stood at the entrance, and two elephants of stone, nearly life size. A separate building at one corner of the palace, with a wide stone terrace and balustrade about it, Chinese style. The windows seemed narrow slits. The entrance could only be gained by crossing a bridge, which ran over a stream of water. For defense, the place was admirable.

Two men stood at the doorway with rifles; seamen from the *Ta Ming*. At Cairn's approach they greeted him with grins. One turned and hurried inside.

"Is Mynheer Vandunk here?" Cairn asked the other, who saluted.

"Yes, tuan kapitan. He has been expecting you."

Inside the heavy double doors, Cairn met the other guard, who turned and led him through two lighted rooms, into a third. Here at one table sat Vandunk and the resident. At another were three natives, obviously men of rank; for them to eat with Christians would have been unpardonable. Native servants were handing about dishes.

"Hello, Cap'n, hello!" exclaimed Vandunk cordially. "Where in the devil's name have you been? Come and pitch in. Been searching the damned town for you."

Cairn laughed, drew up a chair, and nodded to the resident. The latter looked rather fuddled; the bottle of Schnapps beside his plate was half empty.

"You should have looked closer to home, mynheer," he returned. "To tell the truth, I've had a drop too much aboard. When we got here I tried to follow you and got lost. Went into some kind of parlor, curled up, and went to sleep. I woke up and tried to find my way out, walked slap into a lot of native women—and damned if they didn't knock me out!"

He fingered the bump on his head ruefully. The little shoe-button eyes of Vandunk bored into him, then glimmered with mirth.

"So help me! The women's quarters! And what happened?"

"They tied me up and had no end of fun." Cairn cursed heatedly. "At last, about dark, I managed to work my hands loose. After a while I got free and slipped out, and here I am—"

Vandunk poked the resident in the ribs, and in Dutch repeated the story. The resident wagged his head sadly.

"Lucky man," he said. "Lucky to be alive. Strictly forbidden to molest the native women—"

And, lifting his glass, he gulped down some more schnapps.

Vandunk called a servant, ordered a plate for Cairn, then rose. Cairn went with him to the other table, where he was introduced to the three natives. The only name Cairn caught was that of Lop Mansur, Lop the Victorious. This man was bony, unusually large of frame for a Malay, and unsmiling; he greeted Cairn with a grim, intent appraisal not without menace.

"That's the new sultan, Cap'n," said Vandunk. "Come on, pitch in. Council meets in half an hour. I want you there. You've a gun?"

Cairn slapped his pocket, and the other nodded.

"Right. Hang on to it. I've sent for Mr. Drift; going to start putting cargo aboard first thing in the morning. He can attend to it. How d'you like the sultana?"

"The bargain holds," Cairn replied, and Vandunk chuckled.

"Aye, if I don't change my mind. We've got ten sepoys on hand, and six of our own men, and Lop Mansur over there has twenty guards who've taken his money; enough to clean up on the whole damned place. Pitch in and get your meal."

He went over to the other table, squatted on a cushion, and fell into talk with Lop Mansur and the other two Malays. Presently one of the palace guards came in, salaamed to Lop Mansur, and began to speak, low-voiced. Glances were flung at Cairn, but the latter paid no attention. Another guard came in, making some report about Chandra Das. It seemed that the latter had completely disappeared.

"I tell you, we can expect only destruction here!" The resident lifted his head and addressed Cairn, a mournful fixity in his eyes. Dejection filled his spirit; whether it was the liquor speaking, or some inner conviction, he expressed a deep and hopeless despair.

"I have felt it from the first; now I know it is close at hand," he went on. "You were wrong to come here, mynheer. These people are treacherous, and though I have shot many of them, one never knows what to expect. Worst of all is that accursed girl. She is white, and not to be treated as a native. Even if you depose her, how will you handle the new sultan? This chief Lop is dangerous. He is cruel, implacable, capable of any treachery. And we are all doomed. I know it."

He took another drink. Tears came to his eyes and slowly trickled out and down his cheeks, unheeded. Cairn regarded him with momentary astonishment and contempt. Such a man to be a resident, an administrator! Yes; any warning to him would have been utterly useless. The Devil's Bosun would laugh at such a weakling.

VANDUNK ROSE and returned to them, swiftly, and stooped.

"Let me have that Webley," he said, excited animation in his broad features. "I'll get you another later. That damned chief will sell his soul for a pistol; you'll not be needing it, likely. You don't mind?"

Cairn shrugged. "Not a bit," he said, and slipping the fiat

automatic from his pocket, put it into the other's hand. Vandunk crossed back to the table of the Malays and after a moment Lop Mansur thrust the weapon beneath his sarong, a glitter in his snaky eyes. Natural enough, thought Cairn, that such a gift would conclude the bargain made with this Malay chief. A palace guard came in with word of the sultana's approach.

The three Malays rose. Vandunk came back to his own table and looked at the resident. A subtle change had crept over him. He was filled with eagerness, with a breath-taking excitement; his wide nostrils flared at each breath, his mask of mirthless humor had settled into grim lines. Cairn sensed instantly that the crisis had come.

"All ready, Cairn. Council meets in the big rear room; she's on her way and we must be there. Our crowd's all primed, so step out. Wake up, you blasted dog—"

And roughly, he seized the resident, dragging him to his feet with crude effort, supporting him, wasting no ceremony or politeness on him. The unhappy resident wiped his cheeks and stumbled along. Cairn followed. The three Malay chiefs came after him, but first came the two guards from outside. They joined Cairn, one on either side of him, as though escorting him alone.

For the first time, he felt an uneasy sensation, at this escort. Then it passed. Everything passed, except the astonishing scene before him, as a hanging fell away and the council room was revealed.

It is Malay custom to hold audience in the open air. So this room, for floor, had beaten earth, with young clumps of bamboo cunningly concealed along the walls, and vines growing, and even two chickens pecking at grain scattered among rocks at one side. The ceiling was of cloth pricked out with star-shaped holes, behind or above which many lamps were burning. Thus was made the counterfeit of an open-air meeting, light coming down from the stars.

At the door stood guards, and others were posted among the

clumps of bamboos whose graceful slender shoots lined the walls. Both palace guards, and the seamen from the ship. A group of sepoys remained in one corner, clumped there.

A dozen Malays sat in a semi-circle behind an empty mat, obviously awaiting the sultana. Two others awaited the resident and Vandunk, who took their seats. Lop Mansur and his two friends joined the council. Obeying a gesture from Vandunk, Cairn stood at one side; and he noted that the two seamen remained close at his elbows.

"Tuan-ku!" arose the chorus of voices. "Majesty!"

She had come. Cairn was startled by the sight of her. Gone was the white dress, gone every mark of the European. She was clad now in the most gorgeous of sarongs, of embroidered jackets, draped with jewels and pearls, her hair caught straight back, the little round cap of a *datto* on her head. The glinting white ivory handle of a kris showed at her waist.

"Tuan-ku!" Palm joined to palm, the seated men respectfully raised their hands in salute. The resident rose and bowed clumsily. Vandunk sat motionless.

She came into the room. Behind her were two of the palace guards; they were checked by crossed rifles, forced back, led away. She paid no attention, seemed unaware and careless. Cairn saw her face clearly in the light from above, and caught his breath at its proud beauty, at is loveliness which struck to the soul. She came forward and sank down on her mat, the council behind her, facing Vandunk and the resident.

THERE WAS a moment of silence; by all formality, there should be long silence, but she did not observe it. She spoke abruptly.

"You, Tuan Vandunk, seem to have called this council," she said in Malay. "Speak what is in your mind."

That was challenge from the outset. The language is given to much beating about the bush, to soft indirect meanings, to implications. She avoided all this brutally, indulged in no politeness, looked Vandunk in the eye and spoke her mind. The resident mumbled something of his astonishment and then fell silent.

"Very well, Majesty; you have commanded, I obey," said Vandunk calmly. "I am sent here to guide the best interests of your people, to watch over them and to protect them. Things have not gone well. They complain that one of their own race should sit on the throne."

"One of their own race did sit on the throne," she shot back. "He was not taken away by his people, but by yours. Where is he now? Where is Sultan Ali?"

"He is dead," said Vandunk.

"You lie," she interrupted swiftly, without emotion, in cold flatness. "You lie. He is alive. Someone told me today that he had been seen here in the island, here in Coomassin."

Now there was a silence that hurt—a silence of tiny sounds. Breaths were stopped, glances were exchanged. The old sultan alive, here? Ya Allah! But no; that was impossible. Vandunk smiled. He was fully aware of the sensation caused by her words.

"Desperate words, vain hope," he said cuttingly, slowly. "If he were here, he would not long be alive, tuan-ku. But we are not talking of him. We have met here to talk of you, and of another who shall sit in your place."

She whitened at this, and there was a startled stir, as of distaste. Here the white man was coming to the point at once, when by all decency it should have taken an hour or two of talk at least. The Devil's Bosun was enjoying the part that he played, as Cairn could see, but the broad face showed anger, the whites of the eyes betrayed excitement, vindictive eagerness. A keen hostility crept into words and expression as he met the eyes, steady and unflinching, of the girl on the mat.

"You have no right to talk of such things," she riposted with cold contempt. "I was not placed in power by you, but by the council of the people."

"And they have decided to depose you," said Vandunk, and smiled again, terribly. "In this I have agreed, for I represent the power of the Netherlands that protects Coomassin, and the great Queen, the Bountiful, the Most High, who rules that land! Yes, majesty, I have agreed. It is not fitting that you, of Christian blood, should rule an island of true believers."

"That is not for you to say," she answered, "but for the council." She turned on her mat and faced those little brown men who stared at her. Her gaze lashed them, and her voice bit at them suddenly.

"Well, have the forest devils taken away your tongues?" she demanded. "Speak! Is it true that you will not have the daughter of Sultan Ali to rule you?"

Some hesitated, some exchanged glances. But Lop Mansur spoke out harshly.

"You are no daughter of Ali, but a daughter of the infidels whom he adopted. Yes, it is true. We are in the hands of this tuan who is sent to help us. We have agreed with him. The matter is ended."

"And you, Lop, feel strong enough to be insolent?" she asked softly. "Listen to me. Do you think I jested when I said that Sultan Ali is here in this island? Not so. Perhaps he will talk with you, Lop Mansur, one of these days."

UNEASY STIRRINGS, glances, rolling eyes; there was something damnably convincing in her talk about the old sultan. Perhaps there was some truth in it. But Lop Mansur grinned at her and fingered his box of betel paste.

"You are a woman, Amina," he said. "Only a woman, after all. You are no longer ruler in this place, but a woman who has need of a husband and proper correction. And, as Allah liveth, you shall have it."

The words burned. They crumbled her pride; she winced before them, incredulous, disbelieving. After all, to natives a woman is but a chattel, a light thing for man's pleasure, and Malay minds regard her not highly.

Startled, she swept the brown faces, then she turned about and met the smiling evil gaze of Vandunk.

"What does this mean?" she cried out in a choked voice, as though she perceived the meaning yet shrank from it in fear and terror. "What does this mean?"

"You have heard," replied the Devil's Bosun softly. "You are no longer sultana of Coomassin. You are Amina, ward of the government, a woman—who is, indeed, in much need of a husband. You shall have that husband. You shall go with him here and now, go to his house, which is henceforth yours, and be his wife. It is a small matter."

"Are you—are you out of your senses?" she cried, and started suddenly to her feet. "You do not dare! You do not dare bring such indignity to me—"

"Men talk of daring, not women," said Vandunk, and his smile widened. Her torment, the agony of her eyes, seemed to delight him. "You are a woman, and I give you to the person best fitted to cherish and correct you. Lop Mansur, have her taken to your own house, for she is yours."

Amina stiffened, stood staring, frozen, incapable of motion.

But Cairn, who had followed the swift words fairly well, started at hearing this decision. He moved, was about to speak, when something cold touched his neck. The seaman on his right held a pistol against him, the man on the left gripped his arm.

"Quiet, tuan, or I must shoot!" said the man with the pistol.

"Shoot and be damned," snapped Cairn. "Vandunk, listen to me! You promised—"

Vandunk looked up and smiled at him.

"I have changed my mind, Cap'n," he said blandly. That was all. The words, the look, held so indescribable a menace, so deadly a hatred, that for an instant Cairn was thunderstruck. He felt it, others felt it. Eyes went curiously to him. Amina turned and looked at him.

"Oh, be careful!"

Her voice went through him like a knife. The words brought back everything to his mind—her pleading, her reasons, her dependence upon him. "You're the one hope." My one hope, she should have said. He saw now that she was crumpled; her world had gone reeling around her; she had but one hope, indeed.

So he was gripped by indecision, and in his hesitation the moment when he might have acted, went by. Two of the native guards came forward. Lop Mansur snarled orders at them. They went to Amina and stood, one on either hand; the man to her left reached out and caught her kris, and drew it from her girdle. She made a quick little gesture, then her hands dropped.

"Take her to my house," said Lop Mansur, "and as Allah liveth, your lives answer for her keeping!"

One of the two touched her. She shrank from the touch, then walked out of the council chamber proudly, her head held high, and was gone.

Vandunk looked at Cairn, still smiling, but there was no smile in his little black eyes. They were venomous. He made a gesture. The pistol-mouth jammed harder against Cairn's neck; his wrists were caught, twisted behind his back, and a cord lashed about them with expert ease.

"What does all this mean, Vandunk?" demanded Cairn in a low voice.

"You shall see, my friend. In due time."

There was a scrape of boots, a sharp query outside. Into the room came Mr. Drift, glancing briskly around. Vandunk beckoned him.

"Just in time, mister, just in time. I'll send a native with you for guide. Go to the apartment of the sultana, where you'll find Miss Tracey. Escort her aboard ship and lock her in her cabin until I come. I think I'll take charge of her future myself," and as he spoke, he chuckled softly.

"Very good, sir," Mr. Drift said briskly, and without apparent surprise. "But s'posing she don't want to go?"

"Then persuade her—same as you did that Spanish girl south o' Luzon. But don't spoil her good looks, mind!"

"Aye, sir." Mr. Drift wiped his melancholy mustache. "Trust me, Cap'n."

"And, mister, you take on cargo in the morning. You can't warp in close to the godowns, so I'll send one of these native chiefs to arrange matters. The stuff will have to come out by boat, with natives to do the stowing. Watch 'em close and have your men armed. Pour in the stuff as fast as it comes aboard. Don't be too damned particular how it's stowed, either—what we want is speed. Is that fat capon of a Chinaman still aboard?"

"Aye, sir."

"We'll set him ashore last thing. Until then, put him on the supercargo's job he's signed for; we may as well use him in getting everything listed shipshape. And if anything suspicious turns up, shoot first and talk afterward. Understood?"

"Aye, sir." Mr. Drift shifted position uneasily. "But about this here Tracey woman—where'll I find her, sir?"

"I'll arrange that. And mind," said Vandunk sharply, "don't touch a thing! No looting yet. You just take her and go."

HE SPOKE rapidly. One of the Malay chiefs rose, called two guards, and they went out with Mr. Drift, who had not so much as nodded to Cairn. Some others of the Malays rose and took their departure. Vandunk looked at Lop Mansur and spoke.

"If you wish to be sultan, act like one. Make sure of the palace."

A flash leaped across the bony features of the Malay, and he rose, hand on kris. His voice struck out vibrantly; decision, leadership, authority, rang in his tone. A man to command, this; a man cruel, cold, instinct with power. Vandunk had chosen well.

He went out, and the others of the council with him, and the palace guards. The sepoys remained in one corner. The six armed seamen stood about the walls. The resident sat staring vacuously at nothing, until Vandunk extended a cheroot. He took it, seemed to waken from his abstraction, and blinked around. Then he bit at it and lit it, and settled back into dreamy absorption.

"What was it you were saying?" Vandunk jogged his arm. "About me? Miss Tracey?"

"Oh, that! Something—something about the Devil's Bosun," mumbled the resident, and fell again into frowning silence. Vandunk looked up at Cairn, and smiled blandly.

"You hear, Cap'n? Most interesting. A fine story you told me about your afternoon's escapade, too. Unfortunately, you didn't say anything about spending some time in the sultana's apartment, and coming from there here."

Cairn said nothing, but his features settled into harsh, drawn lines. He saw that this man must know everything. No, not everything. That would be impossible—

At a word from Vandunk, one of the seamen stepped forward and handed him something. A cap. Golden oak-leaves about the band. Cairn's eyes widened on it. He started, then his heart sank. His cap, yes. He had not had it all afternoon; not since he had left the Baboo's rooms. He had forgotten his cap there. And now—

"Oh, you recognize it!" said Vandunk. "Perhaps you can tell us where to find Chandra Das, eh? And how Miss Tracey came to know so much about the Devil's Bosun? And how you came to know so much! And, indeed, what passed in the sultana's rooms—something, I think, about the ex-sultan? Yes, my dear Cap'n, you are going—"

He broke off, listening. A shrill, fierce yell drifted faintly in from outside; then other yells. A shot. A whole burst of shots. Silence again, then another shot all by itself, another yell. Vandunk nodded, and cast a grin at his six seamen, who had come closer to his mat.

"All's well, men," he observed. "Nothing to worry about. That is the new sultan putting my teachings of efficiency into practice, before he goes home to entertain his bride."

"You devil!" cried out Cairn, sudden madness flaming in his brain. "Oh, you unspeakable devil—"

Vandunk chuckled.

"No, my dear Cap'n; merely the Devil's Bosun," he rejoined. He gestured to the sepoys, and in Dutch ordered them to take post about the building and stand on guard until his own men relieved him. They saluted and obeyed, grotesque little brown men from Sumatra, with bare feet and rifles. He beckoned one of his own men and pointed to the resident.

"Take him back to the other room, get him another bottle of schnapps, and leave him."

The resident sighed, rose and departed without question, without interest, with a sodden lack of care about anything. When the curtain had fallen behind him, Vandunk looked up cheerfully at Cairn.

"Well, Cap'n! I'm interested in your conversation. What's all this about Ali? And the sultana?"

"Go to hell," said Cairn calmly, but his lips were white.

"Indeed?" The other regarded him with assumed surprise. "Do you think these men of mine can't make you talk? Strip him, two of you—leave jacket and shirt about his arms. Don't loose his wrists."

They began the work. Exclamations of surprise arose, as the holstered pistol under Cairn's arm was revealed for the first time. It was removed and handed to Vandunk.

"So! I see the name of Chandra Das burned into the leather. Then you know about him too, eh? One more thing for you to tell. Yes?"

"Go to hell," said Cairn steadily.

Vandunk looked at him and smiled—that smile which itself had come from hell.

"Well said, well said," he reflected aloud. "It would really be a pity to make you rebellious and put you into a nervous tension, my dear Cap'n. You might much better realize that you can do no damage to anyone by talking, and may save yourself considerable bother.

"Now, there's undoubtedly something to this talk about Sultan Ali, and you most certainly know what it is. You've deceived me; you've known for some time, I imagine, that I was not Mynheer Vandunk—just as Miss Tracey told the resident this evening. I fancy you know a good deal more than you've admitted, about the murder of poor Lochaber and Andrews."

As he spoke, he lit a match, and now held it to his cheroot. He extended cheroots and matches to his five men, who accepted them grinningly. The sixth man now re-entered with word that the resident was occupied with his bottle. Vandunk nodded, and then fastened his attention anew on Cairn.

"You tricked me rather neatly, I'll admit; in fact, I was quite anxious to make use of you. We'd get on well together. You have qualities I greatly admire and need. But, that's all in the past," and he sighed regretfully.

"You must realize, Cap'n, that I've done rather a good bit of work here. Without boasting, an excellent bit of work. There's nothing like a quick, sharp blow before anyone suspects what's coming. The whole place is in my hands now, fort included. The chief natives are on my side. A new sultan will be in power tomorrow. And all within a few hours of landing."

He beamed complacently, and puffed at his cheroot, then studied the glowing end.

"You see, Cap'n, I can't allow this excellent job, the best job I ever pulled, to be imperiled by a stubborn tongue," he resumed softly. "It's really too much to be expected. I've found there are various sorts of persuasions, for various people, but fire is really the best of all. It need not even be disabling. Now, what do you think? Couldn't we get together on this information I need?"

Cairn regarded him steadily, calmly.

"Go to hell."

Vandunk sighed again. "All right, then, that's exactly what I shall do, Cap'n. With you as my guest. Ready, men!"

CHAPTER IX

H E W H O had been the scarred servant and steward Ali, sat over a tiny fire where rice was cooking, and listened to the words of an old crooked-limbed dotard, who had in past days been a great warrior, but who now dwelt in penury, forgotten.

"Here you are safe; with sunset, the men hunting you went back, tuan-ku." The ancient used the title of majesty, as of old time, to his guest. "Presently my grandson will bring news from the palace and the council. Times are not as they once were, tuan-ku! By the will of Allah, plague ate deeply into all the people; others, the Dutch killed or deported. Your supporters were destroyed. Those who sit in the council now are not like the men of our time. Lop Mansur alone is worthy the name, and he is an arrant scoundrel."

"He always was," muttered Ali, crushing betel-paste in a brass pipe and putting it between his teeth. At his girdle was the kris *melala* with the ivory handle. "But in all the island I will surely find men to follow me and obey me."

"In the island, yes; perhaps a dozen or more, tuan-ku," was the despondent reply. "At the palace, perhaps three or four. My grandson will bring these; my son has gone to seek others across the island."

"Four men to obey me!" said Ali bitterly. "And I dare not go seek speech with the sultana my daughter; and that accursed Chandra Das, who worships a cow, must live in spite of my oath to slit his belly. But there are plenty of men to fear me, at least."

"It is rumored," the other said, "that Lop Mansur is to be made sultan tonight."

Ali's fingers went to the ivory handle of the kris.

"Ya Allah!" Under the influence of passion his scarred features, as is the case with all brown races, became almost black.

"And it was to hear this tale of disaster and futility that I escaped, came hither across the seas, risked my life!"

"It is the will of God; what can one do?" mumbled the old warrior. "Times have changed. The young men are dead. The Dutch infidels rule all things. Above all, there are no weapons. All have been taken by the Dutch, all except a few old muskets for the palace guards. Lop Mansur will be given rifles, if he is put on the throne, that he may first of all kill his enemies."

"Perhaps I can find fitting arms for four men," and the eyes of Ali glittered. A swift pad-pad of bare feet sounded. "Here is your grandson now."

A boy of fifteen, panting, came into the hut. He squatted down and saluted Ali with the title of tuan-ku, awe in his face. Ali commanded him to speak, and words rushed forth from his lips.

"The four men come; I am ahead of them. I talked with the

lamp-tender at the audience hall. The Dutch infidel who came today occupies that building. The resident is there. Six men from the ship, ten sepoys from the fort, are there; they have given rifles to the guards who serve Lop Mansur. The sultana no longer rules. When I left, she was being taken to the house of Lop Mansur, to become one of his wives."

Ali started, and a terrible look flashed into his face and was gone again.

"Lop Mansur becomes sultan tomorrow," hurried on the boy, his breast rising and falling sharply, his voice shrill. "An officer came from the ship, and took away the white woman with the yellow hair, back to the ship. The tuan kapitan is there too, but his arms are bound behind him and the lamp-tender said he would be tortured when the council was over."

"And Chandra Das?" questioned Ali.

"Allah alone knows. He has not been found. Where he is, none know. The tuan kapitan ate with him at noon; since then he has not been seen."

Ali's brows were corrugated for a long moment.

"At the fort, how many sepoys remain?" he asked.

"Twenty, tuan-ku. With a sergeant."

"Lop Mansur still occupies the house at the corner of the palace grounds, just inside the wall?"

"Yes, tuan-ku. Tomorrow, they say, the palace will be his."

"You have done well, my son. Now go forth and follow your father and find him; Tell him that those twelve men must be here, not tomorrow, but before dawn."

The boy saluted with upraised hands and disappeared. Upon the silence sounded the asthmatic breathing of the ancient cripple, and the chewing of betel-paste. Ali sat immobile, hand on kris; suddenly his eyes flickered upward. There came no sound, but something moved in the doorway. A man.

THE FIGURE came forward, and after it another, in the scarlet trappings of the palace guards. A third, in the garb of a servant; then a fourth, panting as though from exertion. A raja, this last, one of the council. All four sat facing Ali and lifted their joined hands, and breathed a low, gasping word, both of startled wonder and delighted greeting.

"Tuan-ku! Majesty!"

Ali looked at them and smiled grimly.

"What is the news?" he uttered the mechanical query of greeting.

"The news is bad, tuan-ku," replied the raja. "All is in the hand of Lop Mansur, for the Dutch are behind him."

"Perhaps Allah is not behind him," said Ali. "I am naked; I have only a sarong and a kris. You may remember the kris. It is still sharp. If you follow me this night, the event is in the hand of God; it may be death."

"In the old days, Sultan Ali," said the raja, who spoke for the others, "you led ships and raided the mainland. You were the greatest of hunters; no warrior could stand before you. Then the Dutch and the plague smote us. Now, we are no more than slaves. By Allah, what have we to lose except life?"

The others murmured assent. Ali touched his kris and stood up.

"By dawn, twelve other men will be here; perhaps you can collect a few more. We go first to the rooms occupied by that accursed worshipper of cows who betrayed me to the Dutch, Chandra Das."

"The entry will be guarded by a man, tuan-ku," spoke up one of the guards. "Many of us he has bought over."

Ali only regarded these words with a smile, and left the hut. As the four proceeded toward the palace grounds, a shrill, fierce yell came drifting to them, then a burst of yells; then a shot. A ragged volley of shots, and silence; at last another shot by itself and a yell of exultation.

"Lop Mansur has not delayed," muttered one of the four men.

They came to the palace wall, and scaled it rapidly. Ali the first, displaying an amazing agility. Then on across the palace grounds, the casuarina trees talking and whispering overhead. A side entry to the palace revealed itself. A lamp was burning above the doorway, and beside it stood a guard, clutching a musket, on the alert. Ali stopped, at a touch on the arm and a voice at his ear.

"That man is Kulop, one of those who helped Lop Mansur and Chandra Das betray you, at the time of the fighting with the Dutch."

"Kill him," said Ali curtly. "We must enter by that door."

Two shadows moved forward; the two guards, approaching their fellow. He swung around to meet them, greeted them with recognition. The three figures merged; there was a sharp cry, then the thud of a knife driven home to the hilt. The lamp above the entry was extinguished.

The rooms of Chandra Das were dark, but hunters are used to the dark. A lamp burned in his bedroom, the blinds were pulled, the dining room had been cleared out. Chandra Das was not here and had not been here. Beside his bed, on a table, had been put his keys; they had been found in the dining room.

"Thanks be to Allah!" cried Ali, and seized them. "Now nothing else matters. Bring the lamp and come with me."

In the dining room he paused, sniffing the air, for the hunter never forgets the scent of blood. Then he went to the door in the wall, tried the keys, and unlocked the door in grim exultation.

So Chandra Das was found, and the man who lay dead with him.

"Who can foretell the ways of God?" said Ali, holding up the lamp. "That man was strangled; the tuan kapitan ate here at midday. Ha! Never mind. Here are rifles, pistols, cartridges. Take them. They were here when I was taken away; the Baboo kept them close-guarded in case of need. Take them!"

The four Malays took them, loaded themselves down.

"Now," said Ali grimly, "see that ye get them back safe whence

we came, to the hut where twelve more men will assemble ere
dawn. Go."

Thy gaped. "But you, tuan-ku?"

"If I come not, know that I am dead. I have other business
now. I need no weapon except my own, that has served me well.
Go!"

They obeyed him, wondering.

WHILE THESE things were taking place in the palace,
the bungalow set in its kampong at the north corner of the
palace grounds was witnessing another sort of scene. This bungalow belonged to Lop Mansur, and was his hereditary resi-
dence, being a sort of palace in itself; for he was of royal blood.
His women lived in another building behind, but still within
the kampong.

Amina Talbot looked around her. She was alone. The room
was bare; a jug of water, a Chinese lamp made from the skin of
a fish, a padded mat stretched upon the floor. Lop Mansur kept
his luxuries for external display. She shivered, and seated herself
despairingly on the mat. The two men who had brought her,
were on guard outside the door.

She had been abruptly plucked out of all that she knew, out
of all she dreamed; here was reality, here the end of everything.
What could never happen to her, of all women, had happened.
Fright seized her; she buried her face in her hands.

The shooting and the fierce yells had died away. Overhead
the great "talking trees" whispered and rustled endlessly in the
night breeze. The bungalow, built of bilian or ironwood poles,
creaked a little. She could feel the poles beneath the mat vibrate,
though she could hear no step. Someone was in the outer rooms,
moving about; it could be only one person. The low mutter of
a voice, then another voice, reached her and was gone.

She lifted her head and sat erect, frozen, terrified. She was
still incredulous; she could not have been given to this man like
an old sarong, handed over to be one of his wives—no, no! It
was impossible!

Time dragged interminably. Her mouth was dry, her throat was constricted; she reached out to the jug of water and drank. Still the movement continued; then, so suddenly that she started at the sound, the voice of Lop Mansur came at the door.

"Go outside, remain on guard in the kampong," he said. "I am not to be disturbed. When I need you, I will call."

Silence. The bilian poles vibrated again, though she could hear nothing; the two men were leaving. She thought of the cold, reptilian eye of this man at the doorway. She thought of Cairn, helpless to aid her, and for a moment she trembled. Then the embroidery that covered the doorway was shoved aside and Lop Mansur entered.

HE WAS gorgeously arrayed; she saw now why he had been moving about the house. He wore garments that only a sultan could wear, embroidered with gold and stiff with pearls. In the grip of his eyes was a cruel eagerness. They glittered in the lamplight like agate.

He came forward and sat down on the mat, opposite her, those arrogant eyes of his devouring her in every line. A confident smile touched his thin lips. The cold fear in her face was clearly enough read.

"You belong to me now," he said abruptly. She made no response. He pointed to the gorgeous sarong of gold and green that was twined about her breasts and her hips. "Are you a Chinese woman working in the rice paddies, wrapped up so that leeches cannot reach her? Take off that sarong. You have no right to wear the sacred green of the Prophet—may his name be blessed! You are only my woman now."

She said nothing; she did not move. Only her eyes dilated a little, with anger. Lop Mansur showed his blackened teeth in an unholy grin.

"Sultana no more; servant now," he went on mockingly. "That will please the other women in my house, but you shall still be over them for a while, until I tire of you. Each morning you shall arrange the leaves, mix the lime, have my betel-paste ready for the day—what? Your eyes flash? Allah cast the pride from your heart! You are no more than a woman, a pleasing woman it is true, who needs to learn her place. Take off that sarong as I ordered you."

Still she made no motion. She seemed frozen, except that her delicate nostrils were flaring a little with each breath. Lop Mansur regarded her curiously, and saw how her muscles were rigid, how she seemed actually paralyzed. He laughed softly, put out his hand, and touched her arm.

"You are very beautiful, despite your color," he said gently. "Your face is like a jasmine flower at half bloom, delicate and lovely. I have desired you for a long time, and now—"

His fingers touched her neck, her throat. Suddenly her arm swept out and her hand struck him across the face, the force of the blow rocking him back.

"You yapping cur!" she said coldly. "Don't dare touch me again—"

Black under the rush of blood, he flung himself forward at her. He struck her again and again, then caught at her embroidered jacket and tore it free, leaving her shoulders bare and gleaming. Another blow brought blood from her lips and stretched her on the mat, hand pressed against face, eyes wide and staring up at him as he stood above her. Surprise, indignity, bewilderment at his strength, held her motionless, rather than the pain of the blows.

"Know your master, girl!" he snarled angrily. "Dare to strike me afresh, and I'll have your hand cut off and thrown to the dogs!"

He turned to the doorway, dashed the curtain aside, and snatched up a rattan that was there. Swinging this, he darted back and began to rain blows across her shoulders. With a gasp, she sprang to her feet; but Lop Mansur seized her by one arm and held her while he laid on with the rattan. She fell back against the wall, eyes burning in the livid whiteness of her face. The Malay snarled at her.

"Accursed offspring of infidels, I'll teach you your place! Off with that sarong, do you hear me?"

The two of them stood for an instant motionless, poised; she shrinking back against the wall, he leaning forward, glaring with passionate fury. In this instant, she felt the vibration of the flooring once more and knew that someone was moving about, silently, outside the room. One of the guards, no doubt, listening to the scene.

Then, abruptly, Lop Mansur reached forth, clawed at the edge of her sarong, and wrenched it away. Like a flash her arm darted down. She swept the rattan out of his hands and lashed it across his eyes, full force.

A choked cry of anguish burst from him, and he clapped both hands to his face. Infuriated, she lashed him again and again, across hands and cheeks and mouth; the loosened silk sarong fastened about the slender lines of her body as she moved, like a clinging evening gown designed to emphasize her slim loveliness.

Red weals springing across his bony features, the Malay staggered back and back. An oath broke from him. He whipped out his kris, and the flame-bladed steel glittered in the lamp-light. Then spoke a voice, grimly vibrant, at his very elbow—a voice that caused him to swing sharply around.

"Steel calls to steel, O Sultan!"

THE CURTAIN was shoved back. The Malay found himself face to face with a man standing there, clad in a tattered, blood-stained sarong. A man immovable, whose face drew recognition to his eyes, a cry of startled incredulity to his lips.

"You! Ali—"

The arm of Ali moved. Not rapidly, but inexorably, with deadly pressure. Lop Mansur flung out both arms, and his kris rattled on the poles of the floor. He stumbled back a pace, horror stamped in his countenance, and clutched at something that stood forth from his breast. A small white handle of old ivory. Then, still clutching, he collapsed and fell all in a heap.

"Ali!"

The girl held out her arms; a sobbing breath escaped her. As Ali caught her in his arms, she went to pieces, fell limply forward. He laid her down carefully on the mat, touched her face caressingly, wiped the blood from her lip with one finger. Then he stood up, his gaze fastened fiercely on the dead man.

"You paid too slowly to suit me, Lop Mansur," he muttered. "However, who am I to murmur against the will of Allah?"

And, with a grim chuckle, he began to divest the body of its finery. Presently he was wearing the splendor that had graced the sultan-to-be, and last of all he tucked away the automatic pistol. Then, and not till then, did he draw forth the red blade of the kris, ignoring the rush of blood that followed it. He wiped the blade on his own old tattered sarong, dropped this above the body of the dead man, and nodded. He went to the lamp, extinguished it, and then bent above the figure of Amina.

In the darkness he upraised her, caressed her, revived her and comforted her; tears upon her cheeks, she clung to him, and he stroked her hair gently, tenderly.

"What—what are we to do?" she exclaimed under her breath. "There is Captain Cairn; you must get him out of their hands."

"By Allah, am I to lose my life and all else for a Christian?" swore Ali grimly. "Let him take his chance. I must first get you out of here safe and well, then see what happens before the dawn. We must get back to the hut of old Sri Akob. You know the man?"

"Of course; I gave him that bit of ground last year, for himself and his family. But how about Captain Cairn—"

"It is none of my affair," said Ali. "Men are to meet me before dawn; men are waiting now, with weapons. Now that you are safe, light of my life, I am content."

A GROAN escaped her. She understood perfectly the character of this man, and how useless were her words. Now he was wrapped up wholly in himself, in a gloomy, fanatic, resolve that blinded him to all else; the veneer of civilization was ripped away. His brain was set upon vengeance. He was impervious to any plea, to any appeal, even to that of honor or gratitude.

"But what—what can you do?" she faltered. "What plan have you?"

He was silent for a moment. Then his voice came, pregnant and dark. The Malay mind lends itself to an awful fixity of purpose, beyond reason or logic; the vision of blood seems to wash away every vestige of calculation. The man becomes a wild beast, seeking only to rend his enemies before going down to death.

"The least expected," he responded at last. "At dawn, we fall upon those in the fort and put them to the knife. After that, comes the turn of those who are here. One blast from the guns of the fort can sink the ship, if necessary. With the fort in my hands, all the men of the island will gather to me. We shall destroy every man here in the palace, every one of these Christians, and these sepoys."

She caught her breath in the darkness. A sound like a fluttering moan came from her lips.

"Oh! And even if you did all this—what would be the end?" she cried. "Think of our people, think how many would perish ere this was accomplished! And afterward, blood and fire would sweep the island. You are one man, with little to lose. They have wives and children, possessions, a future—"

Suddenly she broke off,, changed her tone entirely. Eagerness leaped in her tone, a vibrant ringing earnestness.

"Wait, wait!" She caught the arm of Ali excitedly. "I have it! Listen; I cannot leave that man Cairn; you do not understand, but it is so. I know all about Tuan Vandunk, who he is and what he wants. All that he can see is plunder. Very well; now let me take charge of things. You must not run amok like a man mad with bhang. You must not start killing blindly. Who will suffer? These people of ours, I myself. Lop Mansur is dead, and this makes all the difference, to us and to Tuan Vandunk. There is no one else to take his place—"

"Ya Allah! Am I to take orders from a woman?" growled Ali with quick resentment.

"Yes, yes; I am still the sultana!" She flung herself upon him in passionate entreaty. "Do nothing until tomorrow night; promise me! Do not loose destruction upon these poor people of ours, my father! Let me manage with this man Vandunk; I can do it, I know how! Watch and listen. If within an hour my apartment is lighted up, you'll know that I have won, for the moment. Then, in the morning, I will send my old servant, the woman who serves me and who served you, to the hut of Sri Akob. We will plan for tomorrow night. We can take the ship then and go away, you and I and the others. Safety is better than blood. Make haste slowly, for my sake, for the sake of our people! Before you draw the vengeance of the Dutch upon all these helpless ones—wait!"

She felt his rigid muscles slowly relax. But his voice came stubborn and stiff.

"I will not. This is madness of the worst sort. It is true, I had not thought of leaving here, of going away. But you cannot prevail against such a man—"

"I can," she intervened swiftly, eagerly. "I know what he wants; I can use the one weapon that matters. Gold! No, you had not thought of seeking safety; you thought only of shedding blood and dying. Forget all this; think of the future! You'll see. But you must agree to wait, to be patient. Let me take a hand now! If we win nothing else, but win the help of Tuan Cairn, it is a great thing."

Ali was silent for a space, then grunted;

"He is a man among men, that is true. By Allah, it is! But you should get away at all costs. You can go down the island, hide there—"

"Bah! Hide there!" she echoed in hot scorn. "Am I a slave girl, to hide my face? No! I know what to do and I know how to do it; but time is short. Agree, agree! You might kill a few men, and what of that? In the end, a Dutch ship will come, as you well know. If you give way to your senseless lust of killing, you will gain nothing, but I will suffer. We all suffer. The men who are true to you, the village, the women. I can save all this destruction."

He was shaken a little by her words, but his fingers went to the ivory haft of the kris *melala* and closed on it with convulsive grip.

"You cannot take chances with this man Vandunk," he returned. "I know him. I slew his two officers with my own hand; those men, Lochaber and Andrews, who once lived here and served me, and who betrayed their salt, who helped hand me over to the Dutch. Ya Allah! I killed them—"

Her cool fingers clamped on his hand. Her voice quieted his growing excitement.

"That was well done. But now, do not slay us all! Either I am worthless, as was said in the council, or I am fitted to rule this place. I choose to rule it and to play my own part. Let me do so if you love me! Let me save my people, your people. Remember, for the little blood you draw, streams will be shed in the end."

HER WORDS shook him powerfully. His reversion to the Malay, so evident within the past few hours, was shaken. He was again the man who had traveled, who knew the world, who comprehended the terrible results of his Malay impulses.

"Perhaps, perhaps," and he hesitated. "And that accursed Chandra Das is dead."

"Captain Cairn did not kill him; it was another."

"I know. We found them dead tonight," said Ali. A deep fluttering breath escaped him. "Yes, Tuan Cairn is a good man, a fighter. Perhaps I was wrong, my child; he should be saved. But you cannot do it."

"You certainly can't, nor any other. I can," she retorted. "Even now he may be hurt or dead. We must get out of here at once, then separate. You return, join your men, and wait for word from me. I must leave quickly. Where is my cap? My jacket?"

She got her garments. Then her foot struck against the fallen kris of Lop Mansur, and with a laugh she picked it up. In the darkness, Ali checked her.

"Not that one; give it to me," he said, and took it. Into her hand he put another. "You are the sultana; this should be yours. It is the kris *melala* on which the council took oaths in other days. Down there in Java it was given back to me. I bore it here, and used it. Now take it and wear it, for you may have need of it—Sultana Amina!"

A little later they left the bungalow. The starlit kampong was deserted. Near the gate, a shadowy something lay in the grass. Two guards had been here, but now there was none. Ali chuckled softly, significantly.

Then they separated. Amina hurried toward the building with the elephants, that housed the audience hall.

CHAPTER X

IN THAT strange chamber which simulated the open air, where the council had met, an oddly offensive odor was rising on the atmosphere.

Outside, the sepoys from the fort stood on guard about the building. Later they would be divided into two watches for relief, but at the moment Mynheer Vandunk was engaged. As for the resident, he sat nodding in another room, his bottle of Schnapps drained and replaced by another.

Except for an occasional grunt of pain, it was rather quiet here in the hall of audience. The light of the imitation stars illumined the figure of the Devil's Bosun, who sat on his mat, smoking a cheroot and uttering a low word from time to time. In front of him, four of his seamen held Cairn outstretched on the floor, or rather the ground. The other two men crouched, squatting, close by. None of them was white, though all seemed to have some white strain. Their dark features, inclined toward

Malay or Chinese, were alight, with cruel and absorbed intentness.

Cairn was stripped to the waist, shirt and jacket lumped
about the bound wrists behind his back.

"It is a slow business, but there is no haste," said Vandunk
smoothly. "First the chest and arms, then the back. Then the
lower part of the body; you will find this extremely painful, I
fear, because with this method of persuasion there seems to be
an accumulation of pain, a cumulative suffering. Then the legs
and feet, and finally, the face and head. Perhaps you feel inclined
to meet me halfway in this matter?"

"To hell with you," said Cairn, his voice steady.

Vandunk leaned back and signed to his men. The two squatting seamen leaned forward and each of them touched his
cheroot to the body of Cairn, with slow and deliberate touch.
The white torso was marked and splotched with red, with black
ash. Upon the air, even through the acrid smoke of the cheroots,
ascended anew the offensive odor of burnt skin.

A tortured sound, half cry, half grunt, was wrenched from
Cairn. His hair was darkly wet with sweat; beads of agony stood
out on his face. The two men squatted again and tossed aside
their cheroots, whose fire was nearly extinguished. Two fresh
ones, well alight, were provided by their companions.

"Did you say that you had changed your mind?" queried
Vandunk. Cairn twisted his head around, his gray eyes striking
out at the man.

"No," he rejoined with steady force. "If you think you can
break me, guess again. When I say no, I mean no!"

Vandunk smiled, and rubbed his thick lips with his cheroot.

"I have too much experience to believe you, Cap'n," he said
affably. "Ali, eh? And the old sultan was named Ali. Do you
know, Cap'n, I have some suspicion why poor Lochaber and
Andrews died? Yes. Very clever, the way your servant Ali jumped
overboard and got ashore, after telling us he was the murderer.
But you brought him aboard ship. If he actually was Sultan Ali,

you knew it. And in regard to the sultana, or I should say the ex-sultana—"

A disturbance at the outer door. One of the sepoys appeared, wide-eyed.

"Tuan! The sultana is here, alone. The Sultana Amina. Shall we admit her?"

Vandunk started.

"The sultana—alone?" he repeated. "Impossible. Are you drunk?"

"No, tuan; I know her well. She wants to speak with you."

Vandunk frowned. "How the devil—well, never mind. Bring her in." He glanced at the seamen and gestured sharply. "Clap a stopper on that fellow; get him back, away from here. Two of you stand on watch behind me and look out for tricks from this woman. One of you go to the door and don't let her slip out without word from me."

His men obeyed him smartly, dragging Cairn a little away and wrapping a cloth about his mouth and jaw. The others took the ordered positions, just as Amina came into the chamber.

She paused, inside the door. For a moment her gaze dwelt upon the figure of Cairn; her nostrils flared, she seemed to flinch, at the oddly offensive odor lingering in the air. Then she came forward, fastened all her attention upon Vandunk, and for a little while completely ignored Cairn and everyone else.

"This is a surprise," said Vandunk in Malay. She halted before him.

"Speak English, Cap'n Patterson."

HIS FACE changed a little, lost its mask of a smile. His eyes widened.

"More of a surprise than I thought, in fact," he went on, in English. "How the devil did you get here? Where's your husband?"

She looked down at him gravely, soberly. No smile touched her lips, now or later; there was no expression in her lovely face;

her dark eyes held no touch of emotion. She was as though turned to stone. Strangely enough, this very immobility, this utter lack of any human feeling, lent her words an impressive quality hard to describe. It seemed that the girl had fled away and was gone, and in her body reposed an older and alien and very terrible spirit.

"The jungle devils have taken away her soul, and inhabit her body," muttered one of the seamen. Vandunk swore under his breath.

"Where's your husband, I asked you?"

She touched the kris at her girdle. "Dead."

For an instant, she let this fact sink in. The amazement, the quick alertness in the face of Vandunk told that he appreciated all that it meant. But before he could speak, she went on quickly.

"He is dead, and all your schemes with him, Cap'n Patterson. That's why I've come here. I am still the ruler of Coomassin, in spite of all that was done tonight. There is no one of royal blood to take my place. I know who you really are, and what you want here; I can give it to you, if we reach a bargain. When Lop Mansur lay dead, I might have fled; instead, I came here, alone. You're too shrewd a man to choose war and destruction, when you might have peace with profit. Do we talk or not?"

Vandunk chewed at the stump of his cheroot. The situation presented itself to his mind in one flash. With his puppet sultan dead, his position was suddenly menaced. Obviously this accursed girl had killed Lop Mansur; but the Malays, far from resenting the fact, would regard her with vast admiration, as a true sultana. To seize her, hold her as an enemy, would be folly if he could get her to buy him off. What would happen later on, when Dutch officials and soldiers came, did not concern him in the least. She knew his business here and was willing to pay. Good!

"Sit down," he said, with a nod. "If you can show me profit, well and good."

"I can show you gold, if you like, within five minutes," she said coolly. "A mass of it, in this very building, hidden from the Dutch. It is yours. But first to our agreement."

Gold, hidden from the Dutch? His little shoe-button eyes glittered at this, an avid tensity settled upon him. But he equivocated.

"No hurry, no hurry; there are other things than gold. With Lop Mansur dead, who will take his place? Who will keep the natives in subjection?"

"I will," she said curtly. "And you have sepoys from the fort."

He nodded thoughtfully. "But what about your father? Ali, the old sultan? Captain Cairn, yonder, was telling me about him and about the talk in your apartment this afternoon."

The truth leaped into her mind, darting out from behind his bland words.

"Why lie to me?" she asked calmly. "He told me nothing. I could see for myself; you've been trying to make him talk, and could not. Well, I'm here to talk. Meet my terms and I'm at your service. Refuse and—" she finished with a shrug.

"You win," Vandunk said with brusque decision. "Sit down; name your terms."

"First, I want Captain Cairn taken at once to my apartment and left there, unhurt."

She stood, waiting. Vandunk whistled softly, then cast a look at Cairn and grinned.

"Very well; he's in no likely shape to interfere with me for a while. Two of you men take him along! You know where to go."

"And," added the girl, with that same stony air, "if you find any of my women there, tell them to do nothing to him until I come."

VANDUNK NODDED assent. Two of the men aided Cairn to his feet and walked him out. Amina followed him with her eyes to the door, then seated herself on the mat facing Vandunk.

"I am to remain as sultana," she said calmly. "That's my only other condition at the moment. Where is Miss Tracey?"

"She went back aboard the ship," said Vandunk. "Felt safer there. I'm to support you with the sepoys, eh?"

"I'll need no support."

"Very well. Suppose we clear up about this adopted father of yours, the old sultan, Ali." Vandunk spoke with vicious intentness. "I know well enough that he's somewhere on the island. What's his game?"

"His game was to reach me and protect me," she replied. "He is on the island, yes; hiding. He has no men, or very few. I've persuaded him to do nothing, to remain inactive, for the present."

"By God, he's going to pay for murdering Lochaber and Andrews!" snapped Vandunk with emphasis.

"He is not. Those two treacherous dogs deserved what they got," she returned very calmly. "Make up your mind to it. Even a pirate can accept a loss."

The little black eyes dwelt upon her with grudging admiration.

"You've got spunk, you have," he said slowly. "All right. I'll call off the hunt for him—but if he starts any trouble, he'll catch whatfor! Now about Chandra Das. Where is he?"

"Dead."

Vandunk started slightly, and his face darkened.

"Dead! Dead? Did that devil Cairn kill him?"

"No. It was an accident. His body was only discovered tonight."

"Then—then—"

"I know he brought you here and agreed to turn over the cargo in the godowns and other things; money and bills payable at Sandakan and elsewhere. Very well. I'll turn them all over tonight; they're in my rooms now. Also an order under my seal to open the godowns and put aboard what you like. Is that satisfactory?"

The man eyed her sharply, then relaxed. Despite his self command, a long breath escaped him. He blinked, in unutterable relief, for the death of the Baboo had been a shock to all his schemes. A sudden wave of suspicion rolled in upon his mind, and he peered sharply at her.

"Are you lying to me? A little while ago you defied me."

"I could still defy you, and more," she answered in that dead, toneless voice. "You could be cut off from your ship, your men destroyed, the fort attacked. To what good? My people would suffer, my people would be slaughtered; destruction would come upon the town and palace alike. It is not worth while. Much better to give you what you want and let you go. Gold, cargo, jewels—these things can be replaced, but not human life. Or can you understand such reasoning?"

"Yes." Vandunk remained thoughtful for a little space. "Yes, and you are right. But there are other things to be considered; my own position here, for example. I must remain until the ship is loaded—two or three days at most. If there's any trouble, I can clean out your nest of rats; but why have trouble? Call the council now, at once. It's still early. Announce that Lop Mansur is dead, that you remain the sultana with me behind you. Eh?"

"And save your face, I suppose." A slight shading of scorn came into her voice. "You want to see what they will say, what they will do, how they will look; in short, whether they will obey me or not. Very well. The idea is good. Send out a man to call one or two of the palace guards, and I will summon the council. They'll not gather here for half an hour. That will give me time to turn over the hidden gold to you."

He was watching her narrowly as she spoke. When she finished, he made a swift gesture and called two of the seamen. At his order, they departed swiftly. Vandunk smoked in silence for a moment; his broad features were incisive, his eyes glittering. Then he spoke abruptly.

"Agreed, then. We both want the same thing; no trouble. You show a great interest in this man Cairn, don't you?"

His half sneer brought no emotion to her face.

"That's my affair, not yours," she said. Vandunk bit his lip; for an instant, a vindictive, venomous light flashed across his eyes, and was gone.

"All right. He'll get a bullet slapped into him quick enough if he stirs outside your room; see to it," he said curtly. Then he looked up. His two seamen had returned, and two of the palace guards with them, wide-eyed and wondering. They stopped short at sight of the sultana.

"Go," she ordered them, "and call each member of the council here. Tell them Lop Mansur is dead. If they are not here soon enough, I will send sepoys for them. Go!"

THE TWO scarlet-clad guards turned about, after saluting her, and departed at a run. She shifted her gaze to Vandunk.

"Well? Do you want that gold? If so, come with me. When I go to my rooms, you shall have what came from Chandra Das."

She stood up. Vandunk scrambled to his feet, shook ashes from his rumpled coat, and made a slight gesture to his four remaining guards. She observed it.

"No, they remain here—unless you're a fool. We've only to go into the large chamber opposite here, the dining room, it might be termed. Perhaps you're afraid I'd try to murder you?"

She looked him in the eyes, always unsmiling, stony, imperturbable. Vandunk grunted uneasily, and thrust a hand under his coat.

"No, devil take you, no! I'd expect anything of you," he grumbled. "Lead the way, then. The resident's in that room; but never mind. He'll be dead to the world."

She left the hall and passed into the corridor of the building, with Vandunk at her heels. A sepoy stood there lazily. At sight of her, of Vandunk, he snapped to attention, his eyes bulging at her. She disdained him and passed on into the room where the resident sat at the table.

He did not look up. His chin was sunken on his breast, and with unsteady fingers he caressed the bottle before him. He had ceased to drink from a glass. Vandunk spoke to him sharply and he made no response. He was incapable of speaking or comprehending.

"Fat swine!" growled Vandunk, who personally drank little or nothing.

Ignoring the drooping figure at the table, Amina passed in silence to a hideous oaken sideboard which stood at one end of the room. It had obviously been built into the wall and was of massive make, with a large diamond-shaped mirror in the center. She showed an oaken knob in the imitation carving, and pressed it.

"That is the secret," she said coldly.

The mirror clicked, and swung out a little; she drew it wide, so that it stood out from the wall, and stepped to one side.

"Look for yourself. It is yours, Cap'n Patterson."

The name made no impression now. Vandunk, keeping a wary eye on her, stooped and looked. There was a hollow place in the wall, stacked high with gold coins—stack upon stack of them. He caught his breath sharply, a tide of color rose in his, cheeks, and he reached in one hand. He brought it out with half a dozen of the coins and stared at them, bit them, rang them against the wall of coral blocks. They were gold, all right.

"My lord!" he exclaimed. "Why—there's a fortune here!"

"No, not at all." Her cold manner expressed a slight scorn, a hint of disdain. "It is gold, yes, but no fortune. Not a fraction of what Chandra Das had his hands on. This is only a few thousand dollars. Gold is heavy, you know; one man could carry all of this, at a pinch. It is no fortune."

VANDUNK STEPPED back and swung the mirror shut. He pressed the spring and it opened. He closed it again and looked at her, licking his thick lips, his eyes venomous. Gold! It made his breath come quicker.

"Yours," she went on, still with that same hint of disdain, as though she liked to play on this passion of his. Her very restraint, her air, reviled him more bitterly than any words. "Yours. Gold. What you seek most in and from life, Cap'n Patterson. It is your mainspring. Well, there is plenty more awaiting you in my apartment."

It was well that she added these last words. Under the whiplash of her calm eyes and emotionless words, Vandunk had stirred, tautened, recoiled as though gathering his muscles. His little shoe-button eyes held a bloodshot glare. Then he got himself in hand, at her final words.

"Plenty more," he said. "A cleanup, yes; with you helping me."

"Not helping you," she corrected. "Buying you off. Buying safety for these poor Malay folk."

He grunted and turned. "All right. Let's get back. You go ahead—I expect some of your council have come."

She went to the door and so back whence they had come. Time had passed; Vandunk's handling and testing of the gold had not been rapid.

When she came back into the council chamber, four of the Malay chiefs were there already, uneasy, wondering, talking among themselves. At sight of her, worried frowns crossed their flat monkey-faces. She ignored them altogether and went back to her place on the mat, still in that stony silence and lack of all emotion, as though she were driven to what she did by a compellant force outside of herself. So, perhaps, she was.

The seamen stood scowling along the walls, by the bamboo shoots. Vandunk came in, nodded to the rajas, and resumed his seat. One by one the Malays squatted, facing Amina. Another came in and joined them. Low chatterings took place; outside, in the night, women were wailing somewhere. Lop Mansur had many wives and children. The news of his death had spread like wildfire, had been confirmed readily and quickly.

A number of the palace guards drifted in; they remained grouped at one side, but squatted respectfully, their gaze fastened upon Amina. Another of the council arrived, then two more. The number was almost complete. Vandunk lit a fresh cheroot and smoked, at his ease, as though he were enjoying the situation. In truth, he had been rescued from an unpleasant predicament in the death of Lop Mansur; or so, at least, he viewed it. Betel-paste was passed around. The noise of working jaws was the only sound to break the silence. One or two spat blood-red saliva on the imitation earth, furtively.

The last two of the council came in together, breathing hard, eyes driving about the place in astonishment, and then took their seats. The number was complete. Amina looked from man to man, immobile, stony, unflinching. Then, as they waited, she broke the silence.

"Lop Mansur is dead. The kris that took his life is here," and she touched the ivory haft at her girdle. She let the words sink in for a long moment. "Again I am the ruler in this place, the sultana. Is this not so, Mynheer Vandunk?"

The rolling eyes flitted to the Devil's Bosun, who removed his cheroot and spoke with an effort at diplomacy. He, like the rest, thought she had killed Lop Mansur herself.

"It is so. I am but a man; and what man can divine the ways of Allah, the Clement, the Pardoner? The fate of Lop Mansur was written upon his forehead this night, yet we saw it not. When news of his death came to me, I was angry. It was in my mind to send out men with rifles, to put another on the throne, to lay waste the whole island. But Sultana Amina came to me and pointed out the folly of this course. Better, far better, to spare lives and property, and bow before the dictates of the Most High. Therefore I have agreed. Who am I, to dispute the decrees of God?"

Here was something they could understand and appreciate. Their eyes glinted, as Vandunk mouthed the oily words. They watched him, intent.

"Therefore I have decided that, since Lop Mansur is dead, the Sultana Amina remains ruler of Coomassin. Behind her is my support. You who liked her not, will find no vengeance or punishment in her. What have you to say?"

The oldest of the council shuffled uneasily.

"What is there to be said?" he grunted in response. "Those of us who believe that there is no luck in the rule of a woman over men, cannot well object. There is none to take the place of Lop Mansur. There is no one who has his blood, his will to command, his authority."

"You forget me," said Amina with asperity. Her voice cut suddenly, clove through their hesitation and dismay. "When I give orders, they are to be obeyed. Tomorrow there will be new guards in the palace, men who can be trusted. Tonight there were killings at the command of Lop Mansur. Tomorrow, his belongings will be seized and reparation made under the law to the families of those whom he ordered shot tonight. Do you object?"

THERE WERE murmurs of assent, but the brown faces were sullen. Then one of them spoke out, and it was significant that he gave her the title of majesty.

"Tuan-ku! There are rumors in the bazaars and in the fields that the old sultan has come back, even as you predicted tonight. What truth is in this tale?"

Now Vandunk watched her narrowly, but breathed more freely at her reply.

"What is that to you?" she responded, arrogantly. "Were he to return, the hand of the Dutch would lie heavily upon him. He is no longer ruler here; I am."

"By Allah!" spoke out the oldest of them, half angrily. "It is not fitting that the hand of a woman should take the life of Lop Mansur!"

There were quick murmurs of agreement, and hands went to knife-haft instinctively, and black teeth showed in snarls.

Here was the moment Amina had waited; now her voice flung at them with bitter authority and decision.

"Ye have called Allah to witness; well and good! I do the same. By Allah and by the beard of the Prophet, and by the beards of your fathers, ye shall here and now swear to support and uphold me, to obey me, to keep me for ruler. An oath which shall bind you, and not you alone but all those who depend on you and obey you. An oath which cannot be broken without covering your heads with shame. And if you refuse this oath, then look to it ere evil fall upon you and yours!"

So speaking, she whipped out the long flame-bladed kris, the kris *melala* whose steel was cunningly inlaid with gold, and laid it on the mat before her. To Vandunk it was merely a gesture of menace, a threat to carry over her argument.

But to these men of the council, it was something fright-fully otherwise. A sharp gasp of breath came from one, the eyes of another dilated; man after man, they recognized this weapon, which had not been seen since the old sultan departed. And more, they recognized what lay behind her words, her menace, her whole presence here.

To them, this bit of steel with the common ivory haft was more eloquent than any words. For generations it had been the kris of the sultan, the only symbol of authority in Malay eyes; upon it had vows of fealty and obedience been sworn, time out of mind. To Vandunk, to his seamen, it was only a kris like any other kris, but to the guards and the rajas of the council, it conveyed a terrible message.

Now they understood clearly whose hand had slain Lop Mansur this night; there was still a smear of crimson on the ivory haft, for blood cannot be washed from ivory, but must be scraped. All their questions regarding the old sultan were here answered in full, as though Ali himself had answered. To each man of them, this blade conveyed a threat of vital import, a threat as deadly and uncompromising as though spoken from the lips of the old sultan in person. The girl before them was forgotten. She was but the figurehead; the voice that came from her lips was the voice of Ali, their master.

"Well?" she demanded. "Is the oath refused?"

The oldest of them lifted his joined palms in salute.

"Tuan-ku! It is taken gladly," he said, and pattered out the oath, and the others joined with him in swearing. When they had finished, she turned and beckoned the group of palace guards forward. They came, submissive beneath her eye.

"Do you swear?" she demanded. "Reflect well, you faithless ones who betrayed me this night to serve a man who is now dead!"

The guards needed no reflection. They bowed down before her in humility and the oath rang from their lips. Then she made a gesture of dismissal.

"The council is ended. Go, and await my orders."

Guards and rajas together went out of this place as though glad to be gone on their two feet, alive.

ALL THIS while, Vandunk had not stirred. His gaze had been fastened upon Amina in fascination, in wondering admiration. As he watched her, watched the slim throat and neck, the motionless slim hands, the gently budding sarong at her breast, the lovely yet emotionless features, his breath began to come faster and faster. His eyes dilated a little, and color rose in his face, and his nostrils flared.

Now, suddenly, as though abruptly conscious of all that his gaze must reveal, he stirred and scrambled to his feet. He stretched himself, with elaborate unconcern.

"Well played!" he exclaimed. She rose with a lithe flowing motion, a grace, that caught his eye and brought a glowing eagerness to his face. "You—well, you should be on the stage, Sultana. You're a wonder. That bit with the knife knocked 'em cold. Now, what about the stuff that Chandra Das had for me?"

"I think you had better wait here," she said calmly, and for a moment her dark eyes rested upon him as though she discerned some peril in the night did they leave together. "Send two of your men with me. I'll wrap up everything and give it to them. You can trust these men?"

Vandunk looked at his six men—for the two who escorted Cairn had returned long since—and grinned with evil humor. Before his glance they shifted position uneasily and looked away.

"Oh yes, I can trust them," he said softly. He indicated two of the men, who took a step forward at his gesture. "Escort the sultana to her own place, and bring back the package she gives you. And bring it quickly."

"Yes, tuan kapitan," they responded, with a salute.

Without further notice of him or them, Amina walked out of the place. They followed her submissively.

Cheroot between teeth, Vandunk watched her out, his gaze devouring her. Then, when she was gone, he swung around to his remaining four men. A furious exultation filled his broad features and flamed in his little black eyes. A burning energy had gripped him, so overflowing that his voice leaped at them like a whipcrack.

"Now listen, blast you!" His finger stabbed at one of them. "Get aboard ship, if you have to swim—at once! Tell Tuan Drift to get up steam in the morning. At noon, he's to come ashore with every man he can spare, ready for action when he gets here. Go!"

The man laid aside his rifle, saluted, and departed. Vandunk stepped up to the other three, his voice falling.

"You're relieved of all other duty. Take turns, hour by hour, watching the rooms of the sultana. Tonight or early in the morning, she'll send out a message; follow the woman who takes it, or the palace guard. Give no alarm, but bring me back word where that messenger goes, and be swift. That's all—be off!"

The three men laid aside their rifles, saluted, and departed, leaving Vandunk alone. He puffed hard at his cheroot for a little, and a smile grew upon his thick lips. Then he threw away the cheroot.

"Blast you! Now I've got you, Ali!" he muttered exultantly. "You will murder my officers, eh? Now I've got you—got you all, got the whole bloody lot of you. That cold English girl—bah! Let her go hang. But you, my beauty, you with your slender neck and your proud eyes—how could I have been blind to you before? This time, you'll get a husband you won't put a knife into—and by God, I'll break you!"

His fingers, clenching triumphantly at the air, seemed as though tightening upon a slim throat; and his eyes were the eyes of a devil unleashed.

CHAPTER XI

IT WAS midnight before they had finished talking, and before Amina beckoned the old Malay woman squatting in one corner like a shriveled monkey. A French porcelain clock on the desk was striking twelve with slow, chiming strokes.

Midnight. But, before this, so much had happened!

What impressed Cairn most, was the ammonia. As he lay on the divan, he saw Amina come in, wrap up all the money and gems and papers in a shawl, and give the parcel to someone outside. Then she barred the door, spoke sharply to the old Malay woman, and came over to the divan. She crouched there, holding a lamp, looking at Cairn's naked chest and arms, touching the burns gently. He saw the blood on her lip.

"Amina! You're hurt?"

She looked up and met his eyes. She had changed; she looked older, graver, and the light in her face was more radiant with energy and decision. For a moment she made no reply, until the old woman had spread cotton over the burns and wet this from the bottle. Ammonia. The pungent fumes made Cairn cough, until she flung a sarong over the wet cotton, and smiled at him.

"It will stop the pain; I discovered it years ago. It takes out all the fire. After a while, I'll put on a bandage of herbs. Smoke if you like; here are cigarettes and a stand, where you can reach them. I'll be back presently."

She called the old woman and went into the other room. Cairn lay back on the pillows and closed his eyes. Yes, almost at once the pain began to lessen. The surcease was grateful; his nerves grew calmer.

After a time she returned and dropped into a chair beside him. The Malay costume was gone; she was enveloped in a négligé of rippling peachblow silk, and her attitude expressed utter weariness and relaxation. She picked up a cigarette, lit it, then met the gaze of Cairn.

"You're feeling better? We'll have the herb poultice presently. Tomorrow most of the soreness will be gone," she said. "Well, I hardly know where to begin. My poor friend! Why wouldn't you tell him everything? I told him enough, bought him off, and he's content."

Cairn disregarded her words. "You didn't kill Lop Mansur? You wouldn't have that smile in your eyes, if you had. Who did?"

"Ali."

She leaned forward, and with gathering energy began to tell him all that had happened, and how her pact with Vandunk had ended. The kris *melala* lay on the floor where she had dropped it at her first entry. A sparkle came back into her eyes, as she told of its effect on the council, while Vandunk sat there all unwitting.

As he listened, Cairn put out his hand, and her fingers came to his. He closed his eyes, listening, his brain running ahead desperately. He suppressed a groan, as she went on eagerly about her plans. Up to a certain point, well and good; after that, everything fell to pieces.

"It will be so easy!" she hurried on. "Miss Tracey is aboard the ship now. They'll be loading cargo aboard tomorrow. I'll have Ali and a few of his men join the stevedores and hide.

Tomorrow night we'll join them, take over the ship, and sail away."

This was her plan, vague and hopeless as Cairn too well realized. All she wanted was to get away from the island, leave it forever, and take Ali to Sandakan or Saigon, anywhere he might be safe from the Dutch. But to Cairn, the thing seemed impossible. He, scrutinizing each detail that she overlooked, clearly perceived the folly of it, and tried to show it to her also.

"You really think it is out of the question?" she exclaimed in dismay.

"Absolutely. You're not dealing with fools; no one can hide down in the hold or anywhere else—not with Mr. Drift on the job! And he'll be taking no chances. Is there any way we can get out of this apartment of yours, unseen?"

"Yes," and she nodded eagerly. "Have you thought of some-thing?"

Thought of something? Good Lord, no! But Cairn assented, sparred for time, tried to see some possibility on this vague horizon. So she had bought off the Devil's Bosun, eh? That meant little.

"No use trying to make that fool of a resident see the truth," said Cairn, as they discussed the matter. Suddenly he started up, only to relax again with a groan; a flash lightened his gray eyes. "Look here! I've got it, Amina, got it! Thirty miles up the Coomassin river is the Dutch administrative headquarters for the district—it's marked on the charts. Forty miles in all—oh, damn these burns! If I could only get around now, at once! We could be off in an hour. Steal a native boat and go. We can do it tomorrow night. You and I and Ali, and a couple of his men—you see? Get the officials there to swoop down and make a clean sweep of the Devil's Bosun."

His voice ran on, eagerly. Why had he not thought of it before? One of those native boats with the big matting sails could cover that distance up the river, which was navigable, in a matter of hours.

She assented, her dark eyes all aglow at the scheme. Ali would be in Dutch hands again; but they would bear lightly on him if he did them this service. Cairn assured her of this. Any man who caused the hanging of the Devil's Bosun could just about have what he wanted.

"You've got a gun?" he demanded. She shook her head.

"No weapons. Just this kris *melala* and two or three other ceremonial krisses. Must you have a gun?"

Cairn laughed, "No. See here, you're right about the pain; it's eased up tremendously. Those burns were all superficial anyhow—"

They discussed everything in detail. The first excitement settled into a steady assurance; it would work without a hitch, it must work! Before Vandunk even knew they were gone, Dutch launches would be on the way. Police launches at every one of these river posts, mostly with guns mounted.

Now, as before, Cairn felt the nearness of her, the liking, the frank outgoing of herself to him. The radiant loveliness of her went deeply into him; the animation, the steely spirit of her, tugged at him. The world outside was swept away and forgotten, the time passed unknown, as they talked of each other, of lives and wreckage in the past. Cairn poured out the story of his hell without reservation.

"I'll stick to this name; I've made good at it," he said. "I'm known; the other man is dead and forgotten. My dear, my dear—the new self is so much the better one! And we're talking intimately here of hopes and dreams, like old friends—"

The slow chiming of the porcelain clock interrupted him. Amina started up.

"Midnight—good heavens! I'll have to get you in shape. I forgot all about the herbs brewing. Wait here."

SHE HURRIED into the other room and wakened the old woman. The odor of sweetish pungent herbs filled the air faintly; they had been steeping over an alcohol stove. She came back after a little, bared Cairn's chest, and the Malay woman helped her, anxious wrinkled features bent low.

The poultice was spread and bandaged. Almost at once, a grateful lassitude crept over Cairn, as though a sleeping draught had been given him. Amina straightened up and turned to the old woman.

"You know the hut where Sri Akob the old hunter lives, outside town? You must go to it now, at once, in silence. Ali is there—the old sultan, my father. Give him a message from me."

"The old sultan!" mumbled the crone amazedly.

"Yes. Tell him—" and with Cairn's assistance to get the message straight, she gave it, repeated it, until the old woman nodded her head shrewdly.

Then both of them went into the other room. After a space, Amina returned alone. She came to the side of the couch, touched Cairn's forehead.

"No fever—good! Go to sleep, now."

"Where is she?" he demanded.

"Oh! She's gone," and Amina laughed a little, lightly, gaily; it was like the sound of tinkling golden bells under the Da Shwe pagoda in the morning breeze. Here was weariness flung aside, a woman carefree, happy, exultant. "Gone! The way we'll go tomorrow evening. I'll show you—later. My father built these rooms for me, you know, and he favored such things."

Cairn's fingers tightened on hers. "Remember, you may lose everything in the way of gold, treasure—"

"Bah!" she laughed again. "Gold is only metal, after all! Now good night, and sleep soundly, my dear."

She caught up the lamp and was gone, humming a gay little tune, and the door of the inner room closed upon her. As the eyes of Cairn closed, all at once. He was asleep almost instantly.

Sunlight wakened him—morning!

He lay quiet for a little. A singular happiness filled him as he remembered what had transpired the night before; her presence, her nearness, the unspoken and yet undeniable bond between them. Yes, he knew now why he had come to Coomassin.

He looked at the porcelain clock on the desk, and started. The morning was half gone; he had slept long. Then came a bright singing presence, a gay greeting, and he looked up to see Amina, radiant.

"Don't you dare move!" she exclaimed, and coming close, touched his head. "No fever; excellent! I'm really a good doctor, you know—"

Cairn caught her hand, and she smiled down at him, tenderness in her eyes. Then came the old Malay woman with bandages, and she drew her hand away.

"To business! Lie quiet; we'll put the final bandages on your chest. How does it feel this morning?"

Cairn laughed. "It doesn't feel. Marvelous!"

"Oh, it'll be sore enough, never fear; but nothing like it would have been. You'll be able to get around comfortably."

She knelt beside him and fell to work removing the poultice of herbs. The skin beneath was cool and firm; the burns plainly enough marked, the blisters gone down. A cluck of approval broke from the old Malay crone. Cairn lifted a hand and felt his stubbly chin. Amina looked at him; their eyes met, and she smiled.

"What does it matter? Still, there's a razor in the other room—you can have the whole place to yourself for a while, if it'll make you feel better. I'm going out to interview the guards and let them know who's giving orders here."

"Did Ali get the message?" queried Cairn. She nodded.

"Yes. Nothing more to worry about now; tonight everything will be ready. There! Does that feel better? Sit up. Here's your shirt—we'll not bother with the jacket."

Cairn sat up, then came to his feet. His chest was bandaged firmly. It hurt, yes; but the raging pain of fire was gone. He flexed his arms, laughed cheerily.

"Splendid! I'd like to wash a bit—"

"Everything's in the other room. It's yours. First, come and I'll show you how we'll get out when the time comes."

HE FOLLOWED her into the bedroom. Here she swung open a closet door, pushed gowns that were hanging, and revealed another door.

"That opens on the garden," she said. "There's no sign of it outside; anyway, it's hidden by a big clump of bamboos. Here," and she drew him to a window, pointing to a small building a hundred feet away, "that's the private mosque of the palace. Except on Fridays, no one's around there, and it's at the corner of the grounds. Easy to get over the wall there, unless sentries are posted—which is very rare. You see?"

"Splendid! Just like a medieval castle," and Cairn laughed.

"All right—see you later, then!" and with a smiling nod, she was gone.

Cairn made himself at home, washed, and made shift to scrape off his beard with a very dull razor. It was better than nothing, however. He marveled anew at the manner in which he could move about without pain. Any sharp action reminded him instantly of his hurts, otherwise he was well enough.

And with darkness—the Devil's Bosun would be nipped!

It was close to noon when Amina returned, laughing gaily. In the separate dining-room, servants were preparing a meal; the fragrance of coffee filled the air. She flung herself down, seized a cigarette, and drew hungrily at it.

"I'm going aboard your ship as soon as we've had a bite to eat," she exclaimed.

"What?" Cairn's brows lifted. She nodded quickly.

"Yes. I had a note from Miss Tracey; here it is. She's quite ill, some kind of fever. I sent word to your Mynheer Vandunk. He replied that some of the men were coming ashore at noon, and he'd be glad to have me put aboard if I cared to go—"

"But why you?" demanded Cairn. "Why not bring her ashore?"

"Read the note. She wants me to come. I'm a better doctor than anyone else here, as you may have discovered. If she's in bad shape, I'll bring her ashore, of course; we could leave her here tonight."

Cairn read the curt epistle and frowned.

"All right; but I don't like it. Don't get that English girl mixed up in our affair of tonight. She's in no danger, anyway—even if the Devil's Bosun is attracted by her."

"Don't worry. I'll take her some medicines, and if she must come ashore, well and good. There's the gong; come along, we needn't be afraid of the servants seeing you now. It's no secret that you're here, of course."

CAIRN PITCHED into the food ravenously. She laughed at his appetite, laughed at her own, laughed gaily at everything; she was in high spirits, aflame with animation and eagerness at thought of what darkness would bring.

"And suppose all goes well—then what?" Cairn asked curiously. "Would you return here, take up this life again?"

Her smile died. "No. No! I've finished with it all. This horrible thing—well, it means the end. I'll go away. They can get on very well without me. Someone else can be sultan, anyone. I don't know about Ali, but if I were safe, and out of it, he'd be happy away from here too. There are so many places! We'll have money enough—"

One of the servants came hurriedly; men were approaching, outside, with an officer from the ship. Cairn leaped up, made a wry grimace at the sudden motion.

"Oh, it's all right!" she exclaimed quickly. "Vandunk said he'd send an escort to take me aboard."

"I don't like it!" Cairn replied. "Are you sure—?"

"Of course, you silly!" She flashed him a quick smile. A

moment later Mr. Drift appeared, cap in hand, bowing awkwardly. He nodded to Cairn.

"Beg pardon, miss," he said, submissively. "The cap'n—I mean, Mynheer Vandunk—says as you'd like to go aboard. I'll tyke you out, if you like. Miss Tracey 'as a touch o' fever and no mistake—"

"I'll be with you in a moment," Amina exclaimed. "Wait till I get medicine and a hat."

Cairn looked at Mr. Drift, who wiped his drooping mustache nervously.

"Well, glad to have the mask off, are you?" he snapped. "You and your precious Devil's Bosun!"

Mr. Drift coughed behind his hand. "No 'ard feelings, sir. I'm sorry as it ain't true about you joining us. If we 'ad you, now, we'd be all shipshape."

"You will be if I ever have the say," Cairn rejoined grimly.

Amina returned, gave Mr. Drift a packet to carry, shook hands with Cairn, and was gone, with four seamen for escort. Cairn watched them off. He had the feeling of something wrong; he could not explain it. Like a premonition of evil.

He lit a cigarette, tried to interest himself in one of the magazines strewn on the table. No go; he was nervous, ill at ease. He walked over to the desk. Beside the porcelain clock rested the naked kris *melala*, where Amina had left it. He picked it up, examined the blood stain on the ivory haft, the gold inlay of the steel. This thing must have drunk many lives in its time, possibly would drink many more.

He laid it down, lit another cigarette, paced up and down the room with an occasional wince of pain. His thoughts concentrated on the coming night. If Ali did his part, it would be a swift and silent business. Slipping out of the harbor, crossing to the mainland, speeding up the wide flood of the river; yes, the Dutch would be swift to respond, to strike. They'd have the Devil's Bosun caught and trapped—

The tramp of feet, the sound of voices, brought him around,

listening. Alarm gripped him—the voice of Vandunk, outside there, giving orders in Malay!

"In there, four of you. Seize him and bring him out—"

What the devil! For an instant his heart stopped; he did not pause to discover what was going on, but bolted hurriedly. Into the next room, out of here! Some treachery was at work. Perhaps, with Amina gone, they meant to put him out of way!

He darted into the bedroom, shut the door, made his way into the closet. The secret door there opened to his hand. He stumbled out into the filtered sunshine, feathery bamboos shielding him—then he halted. Two men, seamen from the *Ta Ming*, pistols extended, grinning at him. The shock was acute, holding him motionless. No secret about the door, then!

"Come with us, tuan," said one of the men, and thrust a pistol into his back. "Come!"

Cairn obeyed, helpless, raging. They walked him around the building. In front were a group of sepoys and two more men from the ship. Vandunk came out, chuckling, chortling as he saw Cairn.

"Tie his wrists," he ordered curtly.

"What d'you mean by this?" demanded Cairn, as two seamen caught his arms.

The broad features of the Devil's Bosun were wreathed in smiles. His little shoe-button eyes bored into Cairn venomously.

"Pleasant little surprise, Cap'n," he rejoined. "Sorry we'll not be able to say good-by to our friend the resident, but he's taking his siesta. Mr. Drift will be ready and waiting for you at the dock. You'll have company, too. All going to sea together, like good shipmates. And then we'll have the reckoning, Cap'n. You and Ali can hang at the same crack. Ho! Thought I'd forget about poor Lochaber and Andrews, did you? Not much. Cap'n Patterson pays his debts. Take him away, you men!"

CAIRN ONLY half-sensed the frightful meaning of it all, as two seamen caught him by his bound arms, an escort of sepoys fell into stride, and he was marched away. After him floated the voice of Vandunk.

"Tell the sultana I'm much obliged for her trouble. Kind of her to send that message to Ali last night. I was hoping she would—"

Stunned, bewildered, Cairn was borne on. At the palace gates, groups of the scarlet-clad guards gaped at him and his escort. On down through the town. Here excitement reigned, voices rose shrill, the Chinese shops were being shut and barred. The reason lay beyond, out on the old wharf.

Another group of sepoys there, guards stationed to keep the wharf clear; and in the center of the group, being passed down to a boat where Mr. Drift was in charge, the figure of Ali. Ali, trussed up, eyes glaring, blood running from a wound in his head and another in his side—a wild thing captured, helpless, tossed into the boat like a mealsack.

The message! The men waiting outside there who had caught him! Suddenly, Cairn comprehended everything, and a groan came to his lips. The old woman had been followed. Vandunk had struck swiftly and surely and shrewdly. Then Cairn felt himself prodded, and perforce stepped into the boat. Mr. Drift eyed him mockingly.

"Going aboard, sir—going aboard!" he said, and turned to the others. "You men wait here. Man the other two boats, and when the cap'n comes, fetch him out brisk."

The men assented. Two more of the ship's boats lay at the wharf.

Cairn, sinking on a thwart, met the rabid gaze of Ali, at his feet. He said nothing; there was nothing to say. Their own plan had failed. The boat was rowed out toward the ship. She had steam up, as the curl of smoke from her funnels indicated, and had been warped around.

"Ready to go, Cap'n," said Mr. Drift briskly. "But you won't be taking her."

No, he wouldn't be taking her. An awful sense of failure, or despair, overwhelmed Cairn. He turned to Mr. Drift.

"Where—where's the sultana?"

"Locked up, sir," and Mr. Drift chuckled. "She give Miss Tracey some medicine and then I locked 'er up. And fair mad, she was. My eye! Don't you go making it 'ard for me, sir, because I'd be sorry to 'ave to shoot you."

Cairn relaxed, stifling an oath. Locked up! Vandunk had meant his words, then. He was being taken to sea, and so was Ali—for safe riddance. No one who knew too much about the Devil's Bosun could live to tell of it. And Ali would be murdered for having killed Lochaber and Andrews. It was all frightfully plain now, hideously clear.

Looking back, Cairn saw men coming, down to the wharf and the waiting boats, men laden down. Plunder from the palace, no doubt. All Amina's planning had been useless. She had been lured aboard—the note from Stella Tracey had been all the lure needed—so none of the Malays would suspect the truth and make trouble. Ali was a captive and out of the way. Yes, everything had gone smash now.

He mounted in dull, stupefied despair to the deck. His wrists were firmly lashed; his chest was hurting now, the bandages must have slipped. Well, no matter about that! Men were busy getting the forward hatch battened down. Vandunk was not waiting for any cargo now. He had loot enough, he had vengeance to take, his getaway to make—the ship was leaving.

Cairn was piloted to his own cabin by Mr. Drift and two Malay seamen. What became of Ali he did not know. Stretched out on his own bunk, he was secured there with lashings.

"Just so's you won't slide out the port, sir," said Mr. Drift, with a fleeting wink and a grin.

Then the door slammed.

Silence ensued; long, hot, stifling silence. The port was open. A long time passed, an interminable time. Then voices, as the boats came in at the gangway. Above them the decisive orders of Vandunk.

"Careful wi' that stuff, now! Come along to my cabin with it. Get them boats up, Mr. Drift, shipshape and Bristol fashion. I'll take the bridge. Then knock out the shackle and let slip the cable and be damned to it, soon as she comes taut—"

Trampling feet, orders, winches rattling. Cairn lay silent, bitter, cursing himself. If only he had taken his own way, put a bullet into Vandunk at any cost! Too late now. When, after a time, he felt the throbbing of the engines revolving and saw the telltale on his cabin ceiling swinging about, he fell into helpless despair again. The ship was moving, was on her way.

The Devil's Bosun had won, had won everything at one blow!

CHAPTER XII

CAIRN LAY with his eyes closed. He did not hear his cabin door open. Not until a light, wavering step reached him, did he realize someone was in his cabin. Then he looked up, and pallor leaped into his face.

He thought for an instant she was mad. Stella Tracey stood there, clinging for support, her hair disheveled, an open knife in her hand. So frightfully distended were her eyes, so scarlet were her cheeks with fever, that she looked like a different person. Cairn's first thought was that she had gone insane.

Then she almost fell beside him. Her knife cut at the lashings about his wrists—cut his wrists and hands as well. She panted out incoherent words. Cairn caught some sense from them, however.

"—get to my cabin—pistol there—pistol—"

His brain flew awake. Yes, she had a pistol, it was true. If he could only get it! Useless, of course; but he wouldn't go down without a fight, at least—

She had sawed his hands free, both of them. She thrust the

knife at him and rose wildly to her feet, evidently thinking him free.

"Come along, come! My cabin, I tell you—"

She staggered away, falling once, recovering herself, almost out of her senses with the fever. The door closed behind her. Frantically, Cairn worked at the lashings on his ankles, slit them, swung his feet to the floor. Free! And if he could get that pistol from her, he'd not go down without striking a blow in return! He could hope for no more—but this meant everything.

He paused to look for a weapon of his own in the locker; gone, of course. Then he darted to the door, glanced out. The ship was moving. The passage was empty—no! He drew back. A figure appeared, with a quick pad-pad of feet, a mutter of curses. It was Mr. Drift, going rapidly to his own cabin.

"Condemn it all!" came the voice of the mate, surly and angry. "I got time for a drink anyhow—the blighter thinks as I can do all the work—"

He vanished into his cabin and the door slammed.

Quickly, Cairn darted out. He had to get into the port side passage; he did it, sighted no one, found himself at the door of Stella Tracey's cabin. He shoved it open and walked in.

She was lying there face down on the floor, as she had fallen. Cairn went to her, found her senseless; but a fine perspiration was breaking out on her face. The movement, the activity, must have broken her fever. With an effort, he lifted her to her bunk, and groaned with acute pain as he did so.

Her pistol—there on the floor! She had had this one idea in her mind, had reached the pistol, then had gone senseless. Cairn picked it up.

"Blessings on you!" he muttered, as he examined it. Full loaded. "Thank heaven for this much, anyhow!"

Now—what? Vandunk. That was the only thing of concern now. True, he might catch Mr. Drift there at the bottle; still, a shot would be heard on the bridge and would warn Vandunk. He glanced at the door, still open. Then he shot a look through the open port. The fort and promontory were just slipping away. The ship was out of the channel, out in the open—no hope now of getting ashore, even had he cherished it.

And then, suddenly, frightfully, he heard Vandunk's voice in the passage.

THE PISTOL in his hand, Cairn swung around. He could not reach the door; the voice of the Devil's Bosun beat in at him from just outside. A roaring, furious voice, pouring curses on Mr. Drift.

"Get to the bridge, you damned shirking rat—get there!" burst forth his raving tones. "There's a ship in sight coming down channel. Britisher, looks like. She'll not bother us; bound for Macassar, no doubt. Break out the plague signal and do it damned quick—jump, blast you!"

"Aye, sir!" came the brisk tones of Mr. Drift, and a pound of running feet on the decking. Then silence.

Cairn stood stupefied, trembling before the suddenness of it all. An English ship—why, she must be devilish close, then! Probably was passing close to the course of the *Ta Ming*. His chance, his chance!

Never mind the Devil's Bosun now. Never mind seeking help; he had the pistol in his hand. No such chance as this would come again. He must do it, crippled as he was. The other ship must be close. They'd sheer off at the plague flag quick enough—but if the flag wasn't run up? If he could only gain the bridge, hold it for five minutes!

It all flashed over him in a split second of time, sending a fever to his brain. He, and he alone, had the game in his hands now—everything! Let Amina go, let them all go; no matter what happened later, no matter what might be done, here was the chance to win everything on one throw of the dice! Himself against the lot of them. One man alone, and fate had given him the opportunity to achieve success—if he lived.

If he lived! With a hoarse laugh, Cairn flung a glance at the flushed features of Stella Tracey, then jerked the door farther open. He looked out. The passages were deserted. A low murmur of voices came from somewhere; the cabin of Erh Tan, he thought. Bah! That plump capon was of no use in a pinch like this. No time to hunt up anyone else. The Webley in his hand was help enough now, if he were swift about it!

He stepped out aft, not daring to try the forward ladders. Vandunk was not on the bridge, obviously; so much the better. That left only Mr. Drift and a couple of the men to face. Minutes counted now, and seconds.

Cairn was out suddenly at the after ladders, swinging around for a glance. He saw her not a mile distant; a big British tramp of the Carnforth line, black and yellow funnels. Cutting down inside Coomaasin to make Macassar and save an hour or two of time.

Then up the ladder, pistol in hand. The *Ta Ming* was wallowing in the swell that came in across the coral reefs. He was flung against the ladder, sideways, and for an instant clung there agonized as his bandaged chest swept the stairs. Then, a sweat of pain on his face, he forced himself up. From somewhere aft came a shrill, startled yell, and he glanced back to see one of the crew staring up at him.

Stare and be damned! There'd be more than staring now. He was up, on the deck above, running lightly forward. He could see no one. The boats, the bridge house, hid anyone there from him.

In this stark instant of time, his brain worked swiftly. That other ship must be made to see what was going on. The bridge commanded everything. If he could seize the bridge, well and good. In any case, he himself was a lost man; that did not matter a jot. His work would be done. These cornered rats would flood up and take him to hell with them, once his purpose was known. No escape for them, none for him—

THE THOUGHT, the swift calculation, all passed within a step or two. Abruptly, everything came into sight. Mr. Drift and one of the men at the flag locker, breaking out flags to bend on the halliards. Intent on their task, they did not see him for an instant Then, as Cairn checked himself and halted, the Malay glanced up and let out one startled yell. Mr. Drift looked up.

Cairn fired—and missed. He fired again, as Mr. Drift's hand came up with a gun. No miss this time. A laugh broke on his lips as Mr. Drift clapped hand to throat and spun around. Cairn fired again. The seaman stumbled, staggered toward the ladder, but brought out a pistol. Another bullet dropped him.

Damned poor shooting, this! No lack of cartridges now, though; two extra weapons there on the deck. Cairn darted forward again. Mr. Drift was down, clinging to the rail, slowly sinking forward, a ludicrous expression on his face; the drooping mustaches and the red nose, the staring eyes—he dropped all of a sudden and fell and was quiet.

Cairn paused to sweep up the fallen pistol, grimaced with pain, and then came erect to find the helmsman in the door of the pilot-house, in the very act of whipping up a weapon. Every man armed, of course; every man deadly.

Cairn fired twice before the brown face disappeared. Something jerked at him shrewdly, but he felt no pain; just the jerk and the thud. He sprang over the fallen seaman and was at the engine-room telegraph. Exultation mastered him in an overwhelming wave as he gave the signal.

The life within the ship's vitals died out. The smooth shudder of machinery was stilled, and the *Ta Ming* drifted, inanimate, on the long seas.

A glance at the other ship. She had changed course and was heading for them. Cairn knew she had seen something amiss; but she must see more. He must make things plain to her; no crouching here in safety! Any instant, now, the Devil's Bosun would be coming on the jump.

"Face to face this time and no mistake—and fight it out!" muttered Cairn. He had dropped his own automatic, retaining that of Mr. Drift. He stooped and picked up the helmsman's pistol. The effort to straighten up was tremendous. Pain crinkled and darted across his chest. He was aware of blood running down his thigh. But, with a laugh, he was out of the shelter now and going to the break of the bridge. Shrill yells were vibrating through the silence below.

He clutched at the rail for support and looked down. They were on both ladders, brown faces upstrained, eyes rolling, white teeth flashing. No sign of the Devil's Bosun however; that was queer! Cairn began to fire, deliberately; he could not miss at such close quarters.

The port ladder was cleared, then the other. Bodies swooped down, carrying off those below. Men went leaping for shelter. Pistols were exploding down there, too. *Whang!* Something struck the pipe-rail .before him with a vicious ring. Splattering lead cut his face, sent blood down into his eyes.

Cairn stumbled back, wiping his eyes clear. A long reverberation reached his ears, then another; he looked up, saw the Carnforth ship pluming out a long feather of white. Whistling them, as she bore down. Cairn laughed, and waved his pistol in the air.

A BULLET pinged past his ear. Startled, he ducked, whirled around. Ah! No sign of Vandunk, but others were coming, the way he had come, from the after ladders. Two men, darting forward, shooting as they ran. A sheer waste of lead, to shoot while running. Cairn, his feet planted wide apart, aimed deliberately. One of the two pitched down and rolled, clutching at the deck, as though in spasms. The other man ducked for shelter of a ventilator, but fell just before reaching it, dragged a broken leg after him, got out of sight. Cairn laughed and swung around again. One pistol was empty. He still had the other—but where was the Devil's Bosun? The thought tore at him with anxious claws. Vandunk, Vandunk! The man must be settled for good, that agile, crafty brain must be silenced.

At the break of the bridge again. Panic had seized the men below. They were running about the forward well deck. Stokers, too. There was the halfcaste engineer. Cairn fired and saw him

go staggering and stumbling away. The brown men yelled frantically and broke for shelter.

Here was his chance—he could make it! If Vandunk were
not coming up here, he'd go to Vandunk. Must do it at all costs.
Cairn got his feet on the ladder, wiped the blood out of his eyes,
tried to get down. His limbs felt like lead. His foot slipped—the
blood was running down in a pool.

Somehow he made it, stood for an instant uncertainly at the
foot of the ladder, then swung around into the passage. The
other ship was close now. She would attend to everything else;
his imperative problem was to find the Devil's Bosun and settle
him once for all.

Here in the cabins there was only silence, and a red glare of
sunlight flooding the passage as the ship rolled and swung.
Cairn halted, weak and dizzy but intent. Where was his quarry?
Why this continued silence?

"Patterson!" His voice leaped forth. "Patterson—damn you,
come out!"

He plunged at the nearest door, wrenched at it, found the
key in the lock and turned it, flung it open. Amina—she stood
there staring at him, uttered a low, wild cry. Ali was stretched
on a bunk, a bandage about his head. With a heave and a thrust
of his feet, Cairn turned and stumbled away, regardless of her
voice. He must find Vandunk, quickly, at once—he was weak-
ening fast, and panic seized him lest he could not last it out.

A door swung open. A figure stood there. Cairn threw up
his weapon, then halted with a shaky laugh. The plump young
Chinaman, Erh Tan.

"You!" cried Cairn, and caught at the wall. "Where—where's
Vandunk?"

"He is in here," said Erh Tan. Cairn blinked. The other stood
calmly regarding him, then stepped aside. Something glittered
in his hand, glinted redly. On the fine black silk brocade garments, dripped a blacker stain.

Cairn looked. Vandunk was there, yes. Sprawled in a chair,

thick lips laughing, eyes like shoe-buttons—fixed, glassy. A half-dry, welling spout of blood staining his whites. Dead—the Devil's Bosun, dead!

With a burst of wild, uncontrollable, hysterical laughter, Cairn let his pistol fall. The ghastly humor of it struck him like a blow. The Devil's Bosun—killed by this plump little yellow man.

The words of Li Tock Lo echoed in him. "The strongest forces in the world appear the weakest." And still laughing, he sank forward as his knees were loosened, and the arm of Erh Tan caught him as he fell.

CHAPTER XIII

HONEST FACES, bronzed English faces; Cairn smiled up at them, warmed to their heartening words. More bandages. They were talking as they worked over him. He learned everything he needed to know. The men cowed into surrender, those who showed fight, shot down.

And through the mist of English faces, English words, the face and the touching fingers of Amina. Her eyes, tender and lovely, the touch of her lips on his forehead. He clutched at her hand more tightly, held her close.

"He'll be all right, miss," came a voice. "A bit battered up, and his face scarred—"

Bandages over his forehead now, shutting out his sight. What matter? The touch of her lips still lingered there. He thought swiftly of everything; all won now, no going back, enough men put aboard to work the *Ta Ming* into port somewhere—Vandunk's loot all aboard, safe for her and Ali.

There was nothing more to think about, and he slipped out again upon a dreamless tide, still smiling, still clutching the slim fingers that clung to his.

H . BEDFORD-JONES

B EDFORD-JONES IS a Canadian by birth, but not by profession, having removed to the United States at the age of one year. For over twenty years he has been more or less profitably engaged in writing and traveling. As he has seldom resided in one place longer than a year or so and is a person of retiring habits, he is somewhat a man of mystery; more than once he has suffered from unscrupulous gentlemen who impersonated him—one of whom murdered a wife and was subsequently shot by the police, luckily after losing his alias.

The real Bedford-Jones is an elderly man, whose gray hair and precise attire give him rather the appearance of a retired foreign diplomat. His hobby is stamp collecting, and his collection of Japan is said to be one of the finest in existence. At present writing he is en route to Morocco, and when this appears in print he will probably be somewhere on the Mojave Desert in company with Erle Stanley Gardner.

Questioned as to the main facts in his life, he declared there was only one main fact, but it was not for publication; that his life had been uneventful except for numerous financial losses, and that his only adventures lay in evading adventurers. In his younger years he was something of an athlete, but the encroachments of age preclude any active pursuits except that of motoring. He is usually to be found poring over his stamps, working at his typewriter, or laboring in his California rose garden, which is one of the sights of Cathedral Cañon, near Palm Springs.

Bedford-Jones has written stories laid in many corners of the earth, but among his most popular tales were the John Solomon stories which started many years ago in the *Argosy*.